CONTENTS

INTRODUCTION

JULIAN OF NORWICH. A 14TH CENTURY MYSTIC

These prayers were translated from, "Revelations of Divine Love" by Julian of Norwich. At the beginning of each prayer I have quoted the revelation number and the chapter number to signify this is from where the prayer was translated.

Who was Julian of Norwich? Does a 14th century mystic have any relevance for our times? Why has her work only become well known in the last few decades?

Julian of Norwich described herself as "a simple creature unlettered," Rev. chapter 2, but she was chosen by our Lord Jesus Christ to gain a unique insight or higher beholding through sixteen visions.

When Julian was thirty years old in 1373 she was so close to the brink of death through an illness that she received the last rites. But it was not her time to die; our Lord Jesus Christ during this illness came to her with the sixteen visions. These visions showed the extent of the Passion of our Saviour Lord Jesus, the benevolence of God and the Virgin Mary. They gave discernment of the Trinity, the incarnation and the harmony between God and man's higher entity. They gave enlightenment on the ascent of man's higher entity towards God; the different phases of the spiritual sojourn on Earth, God's involvement in these stages and God's everlasting wisdom.

After the visions Julian regained her health and as a consequence dedicated the remainder of her life to God at

St. Julian's. Over twenty years of prayers and consideration regarding the sixteen visions gave her "inward instruction." She then wrote a second longer version of eighty-six chapters "Revelations of Divine Love."

This was the first book written in English by a woman. It is a book that is now read and loved by people internationally. It is not only valued as an important literary work, but as a spiritual Western classic, ranking Julian as one of the most significant English theologians.

To discern why Julian's work did not become well known at the time we have to reflect on the times that she lived in. England was going through an anxious and oppressive time. There had been the gloom of the Black Death, which had annihilated one third of the population. There was an alarming insurgence of the peasants' revolt in 1381. Unguided groups increased the lawlessness against the manorial system through the counties. There followed a hundred and fifty executions. The church was also disliked because it claimed tithes, a tenth of the peasants' grain. The Lords of the manor insisted on compulsory labour on their land.

In the 1380's Wyclif's movement endeavoured church reform. His offensive on church doctrine and its abuses was denounced and he was accused of preaching heresy. It had driven the force of the Reformation. But the church in union with the state still had absolute control over men through their doctrine. The monarchy became more absolute than before. People who defied accepted beliefs were seen as a menace to the institutionalized authority. Personal sense of truth was not allowed. In 1401 a statute condemned herectics to be burnt alive.

The vengeful and absolute doctrine of the church focused on iniquity and retribution, and because of the events of the time people believed God was punishing them. Julian would have therefore received opposition from the church and the state. Against all this background Julian's perception was of a forgiving and benevolent God. She took great personal risk in publishing her works and indeed could have been tried for heresy and burnt at the stake. Another factor to consider was that Julian's work was hand written as the printing press was not invented in Europe until 1450.

The essence of the revelations is God's benevolence to his children that are regarded by him with tenderness, being blameless and impeccable through the Holy Passion of our Saviour Lord Jesus Christ. Our higher and lower entity is totally separate. In chapter sixty-four our Lord reveals that on the point of expiry of our lower entity through death our redeemed higher entity ascends as a small child, in all perfection, and purer than a lily, that floats up to the heavenly abode. Our lower entity that can be harsh and unacceptable is what yields to iniquity that causes us our suffering. Our higher entity being in an elevated separate state never yields to iniquity. Iniquity does not have to be the final stage of our life. We can use our gifts in our Lord's service. We like Julian who live in turbulent times can have complete faith in God with his peace and assurance.

More than six centuries after Julian I was inspired to translate Julian's work into contemplative prayers. My prayer is that they further inspire all that read them to consider Julian's teaching of God's benevolence and that they may transform their lives.

Further information regarding Julian of Norwich may be obtained from The Friends of Julian at www.friendsofjulian.org.uk. You can also write to The Julian Centre, St. Julian's Alley, Rouen Road, Norwich, NR1 1QT.

THE FIRST REVELATION

CHAPTER 4

The First Revelation shows our Lord Jesus Christ's inestimable crowning of thorns and God's benevolence for all creation.

Lord Jesus Christ in your passion, thorns like a wreath were pressed down on your blessed head. This was your crown, which made your precious blood seep from the God made man; you suffered in this way for us.

Lord Jesus, you want to appear to us in your Passion. In your presence there is always the Trinity. Lord Jesus, through this presence you want to swell our hearts with your unfathomable devotion now and for eternity. God is in this presence, our creator and guardian, the Trinity is our infinite devotion, rapture and blessedness, through our Lord Jesus Christ.

Lord Jesus, we should be engulfed with amazement, that you, so divine and wondrous, would come into our presence, we who are so unrighteous in our shameful temporal entities.

Lord Jesus, in this presence when we are tempted, you give us enough fortitude to empower us to defy all the demons of the dammed and every spiritual temptation.

Lord Jesus, you desire us to behold our blessed Lady as she was in her human body, a pure meek virgin, hardly more than a child was. You also want us to know of her insight and devotions. She has emotions of adoration before her God and Creator. We need to appreciate her absolute fascination that the Creator should be born from her, someone so humble, whom God had made.

Through this enlightenment, dedication and wisdom of God's glory and the modesty of her negligibility, makes her a true servant of the Lord. You want us to know Lord Jesus that assuredly in benevolence and righteousness she is greater to the entirety of God's creation, save the greater benevolence of you Lord Jesus, our blessed saviour and friend. Amen.

THE FIRST REVELATION

CHAPTER 5

God is benevolent to us in entirety, encompassing us like apparel, with infinite tenderness.

Lord God, Heavenly Father, with your infinite tenderness you encompass us like apparel, surrounding us, connected, embraced.

All your creation you possess in your mercy, like a miniature, fragile hazelnut in the palm of your hand. It prevails for infinity through your delight; you are the creator, guardian and beloved.

As we are an element of your divine creation, we can only find pure repose in you. Everything else in creation will only give us turmoil in heart and soul. When we repose in you we find our sacred tranquillity.

Lord, you delight in feeble souls turning to you, childlike, unhesitatingly, sincerely. The Holy Spirit has inspired those souls in their inborn yearning for you.

Lord, you bestow yourself in your benevolence, that we may rightly exist in your eminence to your desire.

Lord, you are infinity and you created us for the afterlife, for time without end. You restore us through the most Holy Passion of our Saviour Jesus Christ. You care for us in your blessed delight and mercy. Amen.

THE FIRST REVELATION

CHAPTER 6

How our form of prayer should be, and of the immense compassionate benevolence that our Lord has for man's higher entity.

Lord God, Heavenly Father, you desire for us to have the enlightenment of keeping immovable to your benevolence. It gives you rapture when we pray to you, depending only on your mercy and cleaving to you in the strength of your benediction. Lord, you want us to fathom with steadfast devotion that all we require exists in your mercy, this is our genuine reverence.

Lord, we pray to you through your divine personification, your beloved blood, your Sacred Passion, your revered death and injuries. From the fount of your graciousness is our blessed affinity to you with everlasting entity.

We also pray by your sacred cross on which you died, to your tender mother who gave birth to you, through your mercy they comfort and restore us. Your goodwill is also manifested through the exceptional, virtuous assembly of heaven, by their cherished devotion and never ending harmony that they impart to us. It gives you bliss for us to follow and adore you with these approaches, with the knowledge that you are the tender benevolence behind it. Your foremost way, however, is by our following of the meek sacred nature that you saw in our pure Lady Mary. She showed benevolence, which is an element of our atonement and never ending redemption.

Lord, when we concentrate on your benevolence and tender mercy, this is our most exalted order of prayer, in your grace you descend to unite with us in our most vital longings. Thus Lord you give existence to the soul, you give it breath, to make it swell in benediction and righteousness. Lord your benevolence is so near to our mortal creation and is always prepared to bring us favour. We pursue this now and continually, until Lord you perfectly embrace us in yourself.

Lord, you created our souls in your own likeness; you do not disdain or abhor to serve the most modest earthly needs.

Lord, we are enwrapped and embraced in your tender, benevolent mercy. Everything else will pass but you shall be eminently near to us and forever complete.

Lord you want us to discern that our path will be easier and we will give you most delight, if we pursue your wish that we cleave always to your tender mercy with all our strength.

Lord, your devotion that you have for us is beyond our understanding, in its immensity, its gentle affection, its delicateness. You want us to know this love and to humbly ask you Lord, to meet us in all our earthly longings.

Lord, it is our earthly desire to be blessed by you and in your tender benevolent mercy, you want to embrace us for eternity. This Lord is our inborn never-ending aspiration, to be blessed with you in the completeness of bliss, then our true earthly longing shall be satisfied.

Lord, you want us to be wholly engaged in being conscious of you and being devoted to you, until we are entirely faultless in heaven. For by this Lord, we will think less immensely of ourselves. It will do more to fill us with humble awe, devoted modesty and with bounteous affection for our equals in our Lord and Saviour, Jesus Christ. Amen.

THE FIRST REVELATION

CHAPTER 7

How our Lady St. Mary discerning the eminence of God, regarded herself insignificant: and that the greatest bliss to man is that God, so glorious and divine, is also affectionate and kind.

Lord God, Heavenly Father, you want us to see the exceptional enlightenment and devotion of our Lady St Mary. She wonders at her Creator who is so glorious, so divine, so indomitable and so benevolent. This fills her with a solemn awe, that makes her feel so meagre, so insignificant, so weak, set against her Lord; this in the same way gives her complete modesty. Lord, through this modesty she is filled with benevolence and all manner of righteousness, she is above every created being.

Lord Jesus Christ, in your most Holy Passion you want us to know that so much of your precious blood fell from beneath your crown for us. It fell like a heavy shower of rain, so much that the drops could not be counted.

Lord, through your Holy Passion you want to console us in the understanding that our benevolent God and Lord, is divine and awesome, but also affectionate and kind.

Lord, you want us to have the comfort in the knowledge, that just as the highest compliment a wonderful King could give a meagre servant, by making him feel like a close companion, so you to us, give the same, most earnestly and unreservedly.

Lord, this gives us the greatest bliss, to know that the one who is the highest, the most mighty, the most exceptional and supreme of all, is also our meek, lowly, kind and modest friend throughout our temporal life. Lord, this awesome bliss is a promise of what shall continue when we behold you.

Lord, you want us to know that it is your desire that we

should look for this bliss and revere in the promise of it, through it you want to inspire and console us. Lord, through your benevolence and aid this is your gift to your creation, until your creation is completely restored to you in your eternal embrace.

Lord, may we through an immense in-flowing of the Holy Spirit, through your mercy, our confidence, conviction, combined with our devotion, fully receive the gift of your companionship in our temporal lives. Lord, our temporal life is rooted in belief, longing and devotion. Through the benevolence of the Holy Spirit, may we be determined to the end of our temporal life that everything relies upon our faith. Lord God, this is what you desire to teach us. Amen.

THE FIRST REVELATION

CHAPTER 8

How all that was revealed was for all her fellow Christians.

Lord God, Heavenly Father, may we turn to you with all our strength, enlightenment and lowliness, that in your devoted grace and everlasting benevolence you will manifest to us that through your Son Jesus Christ's Holy Passion so much of His holy blood was shed for us.

May we know that Mary the virgin is his revered, sweet mother; the Divine Godhead is eternal, invincible, all knowledge and all-worship. Lord you created all, may we see that all you created is so minor compared to our creator. May we know that our God brought everything into existence through devoted tenderness and that you will guard your creation in the same way for eternity. Lord, you are everything that is praiseworthy and the graciousness in entirety is God.

Teach us Lord, that our temporal life is so fleeting and that we should worship you more. Lord, you want us to know all this as though our blessed Saviour had shown it to each of us. You want us to receive this with inordinate rapture and gladness. Amen.

THE FIRST REVELATION

CHAPTER 9

Of her humility, steadfast in the faith of Holy Church; and how God has devotion for the companions of Christ; and how God delights in his complete creation.

Lord God, Heavenly Father, as you have revealed your everlasting tenderness, then we are only righteous if as a consequence we have more devotion for you. May this bring repose and inspiration to the humble and sincere person? Lord you have devotion for the feeblest person who is in the condition of benevolence.

If we give consideration only to ourselves, we are nothing, but in the entire essence of Christ, we are, we believe unified in devotion with all our equals in Christ.

The existence of each of us who are going to be redeemed relies upon this unification. Lord you are the entirety that is benevolent: you have formed everything that abides and you delight in your complete creation. Lord you are in us and entirety. You shall redeem your complete creation.

May we, by the grace of Lord God Almighty, have faith that out of his graciousness and devotion for us will encourage us to acknowledge this truth, through the Holy Spirit, with immense rapture and exceeding comfort? Amen.

THE SECOND REVELATION

CHAPTER 10

The Second Revelation is the blemishing of our Lord Jesus Christ's face on the cross, and of our atonement. Also how it gives our Lord God Heavenly Father rapture when we earnestly search for him.

Lord God, Heavenly Father, through your benevolence you beseech us to search for you with a devout aspiration, so that we may see you with the utmost bliss.

Lord, we should want to see you; we should see you and possess you.

Lord, if we see that you are constantly with us then we would have the utmost comfort and fortitude in the knowledge that no matter what happens our soul is secure with you.

Lord, it is your desire that we forever see you with eyes of devotion, even if we may only have a small personal manifestation of you. Lord, if we believe in this way then we will develop in our benevolence. Lord, it is your desire that we abide for you in faith.

Our adorable, glorious, divine Lord Jesus Christ you want us to see with eyes of devotion, that through your Holy Passion you take away the disgrace of our degrading acts. It was for us that with an immovable dedication you went through your excruciating Passion to your death.

Lord God, out of your benevolent mercy you created man, by that same devotion you desired to return him to that condition of blessedness and bestow on him even greater ecstasy. Lord, we were made like the Trinity at our first creation, you want us to be like our beloved Saviour Lord Jesus Christ and abide for eternity in heaven, by the capability of our re-creation.

Lord Jesus, through these two creations you pronounced to come into this temporal life of death, with all its deplorable defilement. You did this for through your tender mercy and devotion for your creation. You became a man as much as you could without iniquity.

Lord Jesus, we believe that there has never been a greater exquisiteness in this world. Your agony, your tribulation, your Passion and your death marred your loveliness.

Lord God, you have shown that you have great rapture when we forever look for you. If we look for you, agonise and believe in you, this is the action of the Holy Spirit on the inborn desire in our soul for you. Through the benevolence of the Holy Spirit may we know the magnitude of finding you, through your mercy, Oh Lord? May we look in belief, anticipation and devotion, so to give you rapture and when we find you, bliss to our soul. Lord, through this temporal striving, looking is as great as seeing. May we fulfil your desire to go on looking until we see you, when you show yourself through your benevolence?

Lord God, teach our souls through the benevolence and direction of the Holy Spirit, how to keep you in its wonder, making us open to modesty, giving us all righteousness and bringing you the most exaltation.

Lord, through embracing you with immense belief, to look for you or to see you, may we offer our devotion to you.

Lord, you have shown that there are two endeavours, one is to look for you, and the other is to see you. Lord, everyone should look for you in his or her temporal life. May we have your merciful benevolence and teaching from your Holy Church to do so?

Lord, as we look for you it is your desire that we earnestly do so and not in an indifferent way, burdened by needless grieveance and wasteful despair. Lord, out of our devotion in our fleeting temporal lives, may we immovably wait for you, without complaining or having defiance. Lord, may we have total certainty and belief in you. Lord, you want us to know that you will show yourself suddenly, bringing total bliss to all that are devoted to you.

Lord, you undertake in a furtive way and yet you desire to be discerned. Lord, you shall return unexpectedly. Lord, all you desire is to be believed, you are our merciful, benevolent and devoted friend. We worship you! Amen.

THE THIRD REVELATION

CHAPTER 11

The Third Revelation shows that all formation is in the enlightened guardianship of our Lord God Heavenly Father.

Lord God, Heavenly Father, you have shown us that you are infinitely present in the centre of all things, giving unification.

Lord, through your premeditation and enlightenment, entirety is under your command. Lord, in your eternity you saw all before the creation, you everlastingly do all that is righteous to your exaltation. Through you Lord nothing happens inadvertently.

Lord, your deeds have been accomplished justly. Lord you are in the centre of all the living things of your creation and through them you do all that is righteous. Lord, you have shown that righteousness is purity and absolute and through everything you do nothing is iniquitous.

Lord, your deeds do not need forgiveness or benevolence for they are completely virtuous; they require no more.

Lord, you have shown that you want us to look at you with all sincerity and see your perfectly worthy deeds. Lord, may we have the benevolence to move away from the unseeing human judgements and look to your adorable and heavenly judgements and deeds that are totally peaceful and rapturous, that gives immense deliverance to the soul. Lord, all natural things have been made by you and they have your impression upon them and even your most minor actions have been carried out rightly and completely. Lord, you are the activist who decreed before the earth was formed that all things should be in their kind and in their position in your inception.

Lord, you never have and never shall alter your steadfastness. Your divine design has been avowed from the very inception. You directed everything so that it would remain for infinity. Lord, you have created everything absolutely righteously nought will diminish. The Holy Trinity is constantly contented with your divine acts.

Lord, you control everything to the conclusion that you design, with the equivalent dominion, enlightenment and devotion that you created them. Nought can go amiss. Amen.

THE FOURTH REVELATION

CHAPTER 12

The Fourth Revelation shows the cleansing of our iniquity with the inestimable Blood of our Lord Jesus Christ.

Lord God, Heavenly Father, you have shown that through your affectionate devotion for us you have decreed that we have an immense reserve of water to make us contented in our temporal life. But Lord, you wish us to make ourselves at ease with you by using the divine blood of our saviour Jesus Christ to cleanse ourselves from our iniquities. No other solution has been formed that you would rather impart to us. Lord, because of your beloved devotion through your sanctity, this inestimable, bounteous blood is an element of us; it is particularly for our rapture.

Lord Jesus Christ your blood flows down to ransom those souls that belong to the Kingdom of Heaven. Your precious blood cascades over the entire world for all that are desirous to be cleansed from iniquity. It ascends to heaven to your divine body; it is in you, Lord you shed your blood as you pray to our Lord God, Heavenly Father for us. Lord Jesus you have and you always will intercede for us in our longings. Your blood streams on for infinity through the heavens, delighting at the redemption of all the people who are present and for those who shall belong to perfect the chosen company of the righteous. Amen.

THE FIFTH REVELATION

CHAPTER 13

The Fifth Revelation shows that the Holy Passion of our Lord Jesus Christ has conquered Satan.

Lord Jesus Christ you have shown that through your Holy Passion Satan has been conquered. Our Lord God, Heavenly Father has Satan's influence secure in his command through the Holy Passion and Satan is unable to do all the iniquity that is his desire.

Satan is constantly striving to be as vengeful as he was before the personification of our Lord Jesus Christ. Satan eternally sees, however, with anguish and humiliating abhorrence the redeemed souls flee from him to our Lord God's exaltation by the dominion of our Lord and saviour's divine Passion.

Lord God, you have shown that through your dominion and integrity you thwart the enmity and destruction of the condemned that constantly contrive and conspire against you. Lord, may we follow your example and desire for us by spurning Satan's evil intent, and diminish his worthless influence to nought.

Lord, you have shown that we may mock Satan and strengthen ourselves and give expression to our bliss in our God, because Satan has been overcome.

Lord, you have shown that the evil spirit has not only been overcome, he is and always will be disdained. Lord, the divine Passion and death of our Lord Jesus Christ have solemnly conquered Satan. This was concluded through absolute determined, formidable effort.

Lord God, you spurn Satan for you see him as he rightly is and eternally shall be, condemned. Lord, you have shown that on Judgement Day he will also be disdained by all the redeemed souls, whose bliss he abhors. He will see that all the anguish that he sent have only resulted to magnify their everlasting bliss. And all the agonising and suffering he would have brought them into, will eternally be condemned with him to the abyss. Amen.

THE SIXTH REVELATION

CHAPTER 14

The Sixth Revelation shows how our Lord God Heavenly Father imparts his three offerings of gratitude to his adored companions.

Lord God, Heavenly Father, you have shown that in heaven you are the highest in your abode and that all the redeemed souls that are in the company of heaven are called to share a majestic celebration. Lord, you envelop all that celebration with merriment and bliss. Lord, you eternally enliven all your adored companions making them delighted with your earnest affability and complete concern, and with the wondrous harmony of your infinite devotion in your radiant, divine countenance. Your illustrious countenance replenishes all the heavens entirely with bliss and exceeding immense blessedness.

Lord, you have shown that there are three divisions of rapture appreciated in heaven by the redeemed souls that have assisted you of their own bounteous determination, in their fleeting temporal lives.

Lord, you have shown that the first division of rapture is the redeemed soul whose tribulation is ended, that is imparted with your deliverance and thankfulness. Lord, your provision of gratitude is so elevated and sublime that the ransomed souls have the impression of being entirely thronged, as though they could acquire no more. Lord, all the tribulation and torment ever experienced by the souls of your creation could not be worthy of the awesome recognition that one redeemed soul shall have imparted, who has voluntarily waited upon you.

Lord, you have shown that your second division of rapture for all the hallowed, redeemed souls in the company of heaven, is that you will impart the knowledge to all that company, each soul's work for you.

The third division of rapture is that the original, natural delight with which it is first imparted will never languish.

Lord, you have shown that you impart all this rapture in a benevolent and enchanting manner. Lord, in your kingdom every redeemed soul's age shall be shown and every soul shall be honoured for his willing work and for the time that he has waited upon you. Those who voluntarily and unreservedly give up their adolescence to you are recognised especially and given extreme, wondrous gratitude.

Lord, however, you have shown that you wish to impart all the divisions of rapture, no matter when a soul of your creation turns to you. Lord, you will recognise even one day's work for you and for the aim to wait upon you for eternity. Lord, the greater that the benevolent comprehend your tenderness, the more freely he is to wait upon you for all their temporal life. Amen.

THE SEVENTH REVELATION

CHAPTER 15

The Seventh Revelation shows how our Lord God Heavenly Father imparts his encouragement through out times of well being and depression.

Lord God, Heavenly Father, Supreme Creator, Ruler of all, we give adoration and gratefulness for your undoubted promise of infinite refuge.

Naught on earth should shake our spiritual peace. Lord, you impart succour, serenity and repose, rooted in faith, hopes and loves.

In our temporal life there is the condition of rapture and tribulation. Sometimes we feel forlorn, downcast and weary of life. Lord, you want us to feel certain that rapture and tribulations abide in love without restraint and you bestow whichever you ordain. Lord, you want us to know that you keep us protected in distressing and pleasant times alike.

In times of tribulation you want us to abide in your solace, knowing that suffering will pass and be reduced to nothing, but blessedness will last for ever for those who are going to be redeemed. May we let the impressions of tribulation speedily go and possess your endless exaltation. Amen.

THE EIGHTH REVELATION

CHAPTER 16

The Eighth Revelation shows the expiring of our Lord Jesus Christ in his Passion.

Lord and saviour Jesus Christ, you have shown part of your Passion near to your death, principally in the change to your beloved, wholesome, radiant face. It became parched and pale with the look of death, until after languishing until death it had the colours of death. Lord, it was such a grievous transformation through your slow, agonising death. The fluids in your beloved body withered and your body had the colours of death. Your entire graceful, natural complexion vanished.

Lord and Saviour as you were suffering in your Passion there was a bleak, arid wind and it was intensely cold. Lord, all your inestimable blood was depleted from your cherished body. The wind, the cold and the agony in your body dried up the residues of the fluids. Lord, your torment was harrowing, profound and unbearable. Lord, your wholesome flesh perished slowly with horrendous torture.

Lord, with this lingering, prolonged, languishing death your body became so faded, so parched, so withered, so gaunt and so wretched that your body appeared it had been dead for seven nights. Lord, you continued dying through this suffering on the point of death, till the most intense final agony of your Passion was endured and death came. Amen.

THE EIGTH REVELATION

CHAPTER 17

Of the afflicting thirst of Jesus, his heart was rending with his crowning of thorns.

Lord and Saviour Jesus Christ, you have shown through your Passion that you had a mortal and divine longing. The mortal longing was caused by the dehydration of your physical liquids. Your beloved body was abandoned, depleted of blood and fluids. Lord, your suffering languished with the nails and the weight of your body. The nails were immense, solid, excruciating and they penetrated those delicate hands and feet. They caused the injuries to unfold extensively, while your body which had been unsupported for such a long time, sank under its own weight. Your crown of thorns had been so brutally and cruelly forced down upon your head that as it bore down, it cut deeply into it, making the wounds open widely in a merciless way.

Lord, your precious, inestimable blood dried around the thorns, it was like a crown of blood, a crown upon a crown. The thorns and your beloved head became the colour of dried blood.

Lord, your beloved body dried through the depletion of blood, the excruciating anguish in your body, your body hanging in the cold air, your lack of comfort of even having a drink of water. Lord, no one imparted any comfort in all your Passion. Your pain was ruthless and fierce! Your pain increased as the fluids dried up and everything began to wither.

Lord, you had these pains in the throes of death and as it languished on excruciatingly, your body continued to slowly wither in the harsh cold wind.

Lord, you want us to know that in your Passion beyond your physical pain there were other pains, but words are completely insufficient to convey them: we cannot speak of them.

Lord, you also want us to know that the anguish of hell is greater than the pain of death because there is only hopelessness in hell. Amen.

THE EIGTH REVELATION

CHAPTER 18

Of the depth of heartache and instinctive devotion of our Lady St. Mary and other companions of Christ and how entirety agonized with him.

Lord and Saviour Jesus Christ, you want us to comprehend as far as we are able, the depth of the heartache and instinctive devotion that our Lady St. Mary had for you. Through her union with you and the depth of her devotion, this produced the severity of her anguish. Lord, you have shown the meaning of instinctive devotion cultivated by benevolence. Your devoted mother incomparably imparted this; her devotion was beyond anyone else as her anguish was greater than anyone else had. Lord, we know that the more elevated, intense, affectionate the devotion is, the more profound is the heartache of the devoted when they are aware of the anguish of their beloved in suffering.

Lord, you have shown that there is an exalted harmony between you and us, for when you were in anguish, so were we in anguish. As you languished on the cross Lord, all heaven and earth's activity were affected, so tremendous was their distress. They knew their God was in anguish and when you foundered they instinctively foundered with you, out of their heartache for your anguish.

Your companions agonised in their affliction from their devotion for you. All God's creation agonised for you on that day. God withdrew his harmony for the universe and his domain, affecting both the devoted and the condemned, so all were in torment.

Lord Jesus, you became as nothing for us, and we are united in this with you, until we ascend into your exaltation. Amen.

THE EIGTH REVELATION

CHAPTER 19

Of the consoling consideration of the cross-, and how the longings in our lower entity have no desire in our higher entity, and so is without iniquity. Our lower entity brings us remorse until we are unified with Christ.

Lord and Saviour Jesus Christ, you want us to know that other than your cross there is no sanctuary from the fears of demons. Lord, you want us to have trust that there is nought between your cross and heaven that can impair us.

Lord Jesus, you want to show us to desire you for our heaven, you will be our blessedness when we ascend there. You wish to impart solace in our temporal life that by your benevolence we desire you to be our heaven, through your Holy Passion and anguish. You wish us to desire you in all our rapture and tribulation.

Lord, you want us to know that we have two divisions to our character- one is exterior, the other innermost. On the surface we have our temporal physical nature, which continually bears anguish and torment in our temporal life. Our physical nature is vulnerable and has unwillingness for the right desires it is this nature that brings us remorse. These two divisions strain against each other, the outward for wrong desires and the innermost for the right desires. The innermost rejoices in an elevated and blissful existence, where all is tranquillity and devotion. These innermost inclinations are the division of our nature that will determinedly, in an enlightened and immovable approach desire you our Lord and Saviour Jesus Christ, our heaven.

Lord, you have undoubtedly shown that the innermost division of our nature has dominion over our temporal physical nature. It has no desire for the longings of the exterior nature, but its absolute purpose is directed at being unified with you, our Lord Jesus. Lord, you have shown that the innermost division of our nature brings forth the temporal physical nature to itself, so that in your benevolent dominion both may be unified in everlasting bliss. Amen.

THE EIGTH REVELATION

CHAPTER 20

Of the unimaginable suffering of Jesus for the iniquity of every man who is going to be redeemed, and how he agonized over every man's heartache and despair with natural compassion and devoutness.

Lord and Saviour Jesus Christ, you have shown your harmony with the Godhead gave your mortality fortitude to bear longer for your devotion than the entirety of humanity could bear. Lord, you bore more anguish than any man in their temporal life could bear and in any man who is going to be redeemed. Lord Jesus, you are the most exalted, divine illustrious king who was debased to nonentity and was most absolutely disdained.

Lord, you want us to know that the most significant aspect of your Holy Passion is for us to discern whom you were who bore so much anguish. Lord, you have shown a degree of the exaltation and eminence of the Majestic Godhead, and the benevolence and sensitivity of the mortal both combined as one; and how your temporal living humans abhor to bear affliction.

Lord, you bore the anguish of every human who is going to be redeemed, and lamented for every human tribulation and wretchedness with instinctive compassion and devotion. Lord, you want us to know that just as our Lady agonised for your anguish, you also lamented to a greater degree over her heartache, because yours was the most exquisite temperament. Lord, as long as you were able to endure for us you continued to agonise and lament for us. Lord, you want us to know that through your resurrection you are not disposed to anguish, but you still agonise with us in our tribulation through our temporal life.

Lord, you have shown through your benevolence that your devotion for us was so immense that you wilfully desired to bear anguish, in particular you yearned to bear our anguish, which you bore meekly and blissfully.

Lord, when our innermost natures are moved by your benevolence and we discern it in this way, we comprehend that the anguish of your Holy Passion eclipses all other anguish. That is, all anguish and tribulation will be transformed into eternal and unsurpassed bliss by the dominion of your Holy Passion. Amen.

THE EIGTH REVELATION

CHAPTER 21

In place of the modest affliction we suffer in our lower entity, we shall discern God ultimately and infinitely in his heavenly abode.

Lord God, Heavenly Father, you have shown that it is your desire that we should recognise the excruciating anguish that our Lord Jesus endured and behold it with tenderness and heartache for our iniquities.

Lord Jesus, you want us to know that in our temporal life we suffer anguish and tribulation, as though we are dying with you on your cross. If we, however, remain with you in faith until the end of our life, then with your benevolence and blessing we shall pass from this life to heaven. There won't be an instant before we shall see your countenance of exaltation and we shall be in our eternal bliss.

In our temporal life we have anguish because of our imperfections. In your graciousness you desire to lift us from this to be with you in your exaltation. After our small degree of anguish here, we shall finally discern our Lord God, Heavenly Father, for eternity- and this won't occur without that anguish. The more grievous that our anguish is with you Lord Jesus, the more exalted will be our eminence with you in your dominion of heaven. Amen.

THE NINTH REVELATION

CHAPTER 22

The Ninth Revelation shows the benevolence for mankind that brought our Lord Jesus Christ to his Passion and how this is spread throughout the heavens.

Lord and Saviour Jesus Christ, you want us to know that it is an abiding rapture for you to have endured the anguish for us. Lord, you have shown that if you could have endured more for us you would have done so.

Lord Jesus, you have shown our Lord God in heaven, not in any incarnate way, but in his temperament and undertaking. Lord God, Heavenly Father, you undertake to honour our Lord and Saviour Jesus Christ. This honour, this offering gives Jesus so abundant a rapture, that he desires nothing else. Lord God, you have rapture with everything that Jesus has done for our redemption. Lord Jesus, you redeemed us through your Holy Passion and we are a benevolent offering to you from our Heavenly Father, we have a kinship with you. We are your bliss, your honour, and your exaltation. It is an incomparable amazement, a total rapture that we are Jesus' eternal crowns. Lord Jesus, because of this infinite rapture you disregard all your torment and grievous anguish, your excruciating and humiliating death.

Lord Jesus, you want us to know that if you could have endured any more anguish for us you would have done so. Your devotion for us would have given you no repose until you had completed any more that needed to be done. Lord, it would be above our discernment to know how many times you would have died for us. Lord Jesus, because of your devotion for us you would have disregarded how many times you had to die for us and counted it as nought. Set against your infinite devotion everything else appears insignificant.

Lord, although your beloved body could only endure the anguish once, in your benevolence you would have carried on sacrificing yourself. Lord, with no difficulty you could create new heavens and a new earth for us and count it as a small offering. But to be prepared to die for us so often is above our discernment- that is it is an immeasurable gift of devotion that you offer to our souls.

Lord Jesus, you have shown that your devotion, which desired you to endure your Holy Passion, is far beyond your anguish, as far as heaven is above the earth. Lord, your Holy Passion was an eminent, elevated, eternal achievement of pure devotion. Lord God, Heavenly Father, this achievement for our redemption was determined as profoundly for us as you could, through your benevolent desire. Lord Jesus, you want us to know that your absolute bliss would not have been complete if our redemption could have been achieved in a greater way. Amen.

THE NINTH REVELATION

CHAPTER 23

How Christ desires that we have immense bliss with him in our atonement and that we seek blessing of him that we may do so.

Lord and Saviour Jesus Christ, you have shown the bliss and delight of our Lord God, Heavenly Father in heaven; your exaltation in heaven; and the everlasting rapture of the Holy Spirit in heaven.

Lord Jesus, you have shown through the achievement of your Holy Passion your contentment, bliss and delight.

Lord God, Heavenly Father, you have shown that it is your desire that we share devout rapture with our Lord Jesus in our redemption. Lord, in our temporal life by your benevolence, you desire for us to find immense encouragement and fortitude, to be perfectly absorbed in our redemption. Lord, you want us to know that you find eternal rapture in us and through your benevolence we shall have that rapture in you.

Lord Jesus, it took from your personification to your divine resurrection to deliver our atonement, which was priceless and overwhelming, nothing else you ever achieve for us will compare to this gift.

Lord Jesus, you have shown that it is your desire that we discern the rapture of the divine Trinity over our redemption and through your benevolence we should share in that sacred rapture. Lord, it is your desire that as far as it is attainable for us in our temporal life, the bliss we have over our redemption should resemble your bliss for our redemption.

Lord, all the Holy Trinity was concerned in your Holy Passion, but you alone endured the anguish. The divine Trinity eternally delights that you have bestowed bounteous righteousness and abounding benevolence through the achievement of your Holy Passion. Lord, you have shown that through all your anguish you wished to impart bliss to us and you desire no other reward.

Lord, you have the temperament of cheerfully bestowing to us your gift. You give small consideration to what you have bestowed. Your absolute intention and wish is to delight and content us through the bestowing of your gift of redemption. If we receive this gift gracefully and thankfully then this is your immense reward.

Lord, you have imparted the elevation of your devotion for our redemption, and the manifold exaltations that proceed from your Holy Passion. The exaltations are that the act has been achieved and the anguish is over; and that you have redeemed us from hell. Amen.

THE TENTH REVELATION

CHAPTER 24

The Tenth Revelation shows that our Lord Jesus Christ's heart was sundered in two for the benevolence of mankind.

Lord Jesus Christ, you have shown that you contemplate your wounded side with bliss. Lord, you want us to know that in your side there is an adorable heavenly abode, vast enough for every person who is going to be redeemed to have tranquillity in serenity and benevolence. You want us to remember your inestimable blood and water that you suffered to cascade out- all through your devotion for us. Lord, you have shown that your sacred heart was sundered in two.

Lord, you have shown a degree of the divine Godhead and wish our souls to discern on the everlasting devotion that shall abide for eternity.

Lord Jesus, you want us to discern the bliss and rapture

that our redemption gives you, and discern our God, our maker, our endless bliss, and share with you the exultation of your devotion.

Lord, you want us to discern the depth of your devotion before your death by your will to endure anguish and death for us. Now your entire harsh affliction, all your unyielding purpose has transformed into everlasting bliss and blessedness for you and for all the souls you shall redeem. Lord, you want us to know that you shall gracefully bestow whatever we beseech you, that delights you. Lord, your rapture is in our redeemed righteousness, in our eternal bliss and blessedness with you.

Lord, through this discernment you want to impart contentment and exuberance. Amen.

THE ELEVENTH REVELATION

CHAPTER 25

The Eleventh Revelation is a beholding of Mary, the sanctified Mother of our Lord Jesus Christ.

Our beloved Lord Jesus, you have shown that you wish us to recognise that as you looked down during your Holy Passion our Lady was standing there.

Lord, you want us to know that you are quite enlightened of the degree that we would like to see your divine Mother. After you, sweet Jesus, she is the most exalted rapture that you could impart to us. She is your inestimable pleasure and exaltation and it is she whom all your revered living souls wish to behold.

Lord, you have shown that our Lady St Mary, this tender virgin, is incomparably happy through your unequalled, eminent, astounding devotion for her. Lord, you want us to share in your delight of your devotion for her and her devotion for you.

Lord, you desire all the souls you are going to redeem to discern this. Lord, you desire that we behold through her, the degree of your devotion for us. For your devotion for us, you elevated her and enabled her to be so eminent. This gives you great rapture and you desire us to share in that rapture. Besides you Lord, she is the most adorable of visions.

Lord, you want to teach us not to desire her incarnate nearness in our temporal life. You desire us to aspire to the righteousness of her divine soul- her dedication, her enlightenment, and her devotion- so that we may discern to comprehend ourselves, and solemnly be in awe of our Lord God, Heavenly Father.

Lord, you have shown our Lady St Mary transformed from the humble and unadorned to the elevated, eminent and honoured, who is more agreeable to you than any other creatures.

Lord, to help us discern this more you have shown the example: a mortal who is devoted to another individual beyond all remaining, will desire each person to be devoted to and delight in that person whom he is so devoted to. Amen.

THE TWELFTH REVELATION

CHAPTER 26

The Twelfth Revelation shows the exaltation of our Lord Jesus Christ.

Lord Jesus, you have benevolently taught that we can never find true repose until we abide with you, accepting that you are the profusion of bliss, pure affability, kindness, unsurpassed happiness and existence itself.

Lord, you have shown that you are the greatest, whom we should have devotion for. Lord, we should delight in you; we should wait upon you, as you are the one we yearn for. Lord, you should be all our desire. Lord, the Holy Church exhorts and directs us about you.

Lord, this discernment of you is the most exalted that could be shown to us. The bliss in the teaching of you exceeds anything our character or the soul could aspire to. Lord, may each individual receive this teaching with discernment, through your benevolence, for their perception and devotion. Amen.

THE THIRTENTH REVELATION

CHAPTER 27

The Thirteenth Revelation shows God imparted an immense undertaking to redress our iniquity that hinders us, and that he will make things all things agreeable.

Lord Jesus, you have shown that mainly it is our iniquity that prevents us in our desire to perceive you.

Lord, you have taught that iniquity is inescapable, but that all will be agreeable, and every aspect will be agreeable.

Lord, you have shown in iniquity all that is habitually not agreeable. Lord, because of iniquity, through your Holy Passion you suffered the wretched degradation and complete self-depletion, in your personification and your death. You showed all the incarnate and divine affliction of your world. We have all encountered some degradation through iniquity, we shall continue to know it until we are totally purified by you Lord, our master Jesus. This shall only occur when our temporal body and all our base inmost appetites are totally extinct.

Lord, you want us to discern all the anguish that ever was or ever will be, was not as profound or as grave as the anguish of your Holy Passion.

Lord, you want us to discern that we cannot see iniquity itself. You have shown that iniquity has no entity or materiality and can only be discerned through the anguish it creates. Through this brief anguish we understand ourselves and seek for forgiveness, then we are absolved. Lord, it is your benevolent desire that we take comfort from your Holy Passion through all our trials and tribulations. Lord, through your affectionate devotion for all that are going to be redeemed you promptly and gently encourage us. Lord, you show that iniquity is the creator of all this anguish, but all will be agreeable, and every aspect will be agreeable.

Lord, you show this compassionately, without any condemnation of any individual who is going to be redeemed. Through this teaching Lord Jesus, you want us to discern that in God there is concealed an incomprehensible enigma concerning the origin of iniquity. When we are enfolded with God in heaven, he shall truly discern why he permitted iniquity to occur.

Lord God, as in your compassionate benevolence you do not condemn us in our iniquity, you would not desire for us in our finite mortal mind to challenge or reproach you as to why iniquity occurred in this world. Rather, Lord, you have shown that you would desire for us to wait until we are in heaven, when you shall discern all to us and we shall be in our eternal bliss with you. Amen.

THE THIRTEENTH REVELATION

CHAPTER 28

How every instinctive benevolent emotion of tenderness that a man has for his companion Christians is Jesus in him.

Lord Jesus Christ you have shown that you have sympathy for us in our iniquity, through your precious devotion for those who are going to be redeemed. In this temporal life our Lord God's servants and the Holy Church will be distressed with affliction, heartache, adversity, like a garment waved in a current of air.

Lord, you have shown that you will convert this into something exalted, into eternal blessing and infinite bliss.

Lord, you want us to discern why you delight with tenderness and sympathy over the afflictions of your servants. Lord, to arrange that your devoted souls come into your eternal exaltation, we all have iniquity that you do not condemn us for, but which causes us by the world to be condemned, disdained, held in contempt, ridiculed and cast aside. Lord, you arrange this to defend us against the futile vainglory and arrogance of this inferior temporal existence, to arrange for us to pass into heaven, into eternal exaltation. Lord Jesus, you have taught that you will totally separate us from our futile desires and worthless arrogance, congregating us to make us tender and meek, undefiled and righteous, through our harmony with you.

Lord, you have shown that every spontaneous, devoted inclination of tenderness that an individual has for an equal Christian, are you in us.

Lord, just as you showed how you depleted yourself in your Holy Passion, so you depleted yourself in this sympathy. Lord, you have taught that this not only brings us into exaltation that you desire us to delight in, but there is solace for us in our anguish. Lord, you want us to discern that through the dominion of your Holy Passion, this will be transformed into exaltation and put into benevolent service. We are not in tribulation alone, but you are beside us. Lord, you also want us to discern that you are our foundation, that your afflictions and humiliation are inestimably more grievous than anything we can endure.

Lord, as we discern all this may we restrain from grieving and being broken-hearted about our own anguishes. Our iniquity completely justifies the anguish but this devotion absolves us. In your infinite benevolence you cast aside all our condemnation and behold us with profound consideration and compassion as your righteous and blessed children. Amen.

THE THIRTEENTH REVELATION

CHAPTER 29

How Adam's iniquity was the most immense, but the exalted recompense for iniquity brings deeper bliss and devotion to God than Adam's iniquity has brought to him.

Lord Jesus Christ, we may question how can all be agreeable considering the immense affliction that iniquity has caused your living souls?

Lord, you have shown that the gravest iniquity that has ever been committed or ever will be committed was Adam's iniquity, Lord, you have shown that this is the accepted discernment of the complete Holy Church. Lord, you have taught that you desire us to behold the exalted recompense you have achieved for iniquity.

Lord, this penance has brought our Lord God, Heavenly Father, deeper bliss and devotion than Adam's iniquity has brought him. Our divine Lord, you have shown that you desire us to give precise consideration to this. Lord, you have taught that as you have recompensed the gravest iniquity, we can discern that you will recompense all slighter iniquities. Amen.

THE THIRTEENTH REVELATION

CHAPTER 30

The two features of truth; one revealed: our Saviour and redemption; one concealed and shut off from us, is the entirety save our redemption.

Lord and Saviour Jesus Christ, you have taught that there are two features that you wish us to discern. The first is our Saviour and redemption. This is revealed and pronounced, adorable and illuminated, and infinite for all the souls of benevolence, now and for the time to come, who are embraced. Our Lord God, Heavenly Father, you secure us to this fact, you guide us, urge us and show us discernment, in our inmost heart by the Holy Spirit and externally by Holy Church, in your same benevolence. Lord God, you desire that we should immerse ourselves with this feature of this fact, delighting in you, as you delight in us. Lord, the more we are immersed in this fact, with devout lowliness, the more appreciation we receive from you, and the more we shall acquire. Through this, in a way, we delight in our part with you, Lord.

Lord God, the other feature that is concealed from us and shut off from us, is the entirety save our redemption. Lord God, it is your desire that we be dutiful and revered servants, by obediently not intruding into those enigmas that are associated with your hidden knowledge.

Lord, you show your sympathy for those souls who are so concerned with all these hidden enigmas. Lord, may they know how much they could delight you and lift this burden from themselves, by discontinuing to intrude? Lord, you have shown that the saintly company of heaven only desire to discern what delights you to teach them, their devotion and what they aspire to are dependent solely on your direction. Lord, ours should be in harmony with this. Lord, as we are all united in your perception with the saintly company of heaven may we yearn and aspire to your direction in our temporal lives?

Lord God, Heavenly Father, you have benevolently taught through this, that we should have conviction and delight in our blessed Saviour Jesus, in entirety. Amen.

THE THIRTEENTH REVELATION

CHAPTER 31

Of the devotional yearning of Christ which has been in him from the beginning, and will not be concluded until we are redeemed on Judgement Day and behold him.

Lord Jesus Christ, you have very reassuringly taught that all will be agreeable. Lord, you have shown that this will all be brought about through our Lord God, Heavenly Father, through you as the Son of God; through the divine Trinity; through the harmony of the blessed souls that will be redeemed in the divine Trinity. Through all this Lord God, you desire to embrace us in tranquillity and harmony.

Lord Jesus, you have shown that your devotional yearning will not be concluded until we are redeemed on Judgement Day and we behold you. Some of us who are going to be redeemed remain here, other souls will follow us until they are redeemed and are your delight and blessedness on Judgement Day. Lord, your devotional yearning is for all souls to be absolutely complete and in harmony with you, to your eternal exaltation. We shall remain incomplete until that day.

Lord Jesus, you have taught us, as the Christian faith

has taught us, that you are both God and man. Lord, you have shown that you are the one who is the most exalted and as God you have unsurpassed bliss, as it was in the beginning and shall be for eternity. Your never-ending bliss cannot be added to or diminished.

Lord Jesus, as Man our belief gives us discernment, as God has shown, that by the dominion of God you bore anguish and your Passion. You died for us through your devotion for us, to bring us into your exaltation. Lord, you delight in the achievement of your humanity and we are your bliss, your honour, your exaltation and your crown.

Lord Jesus, as our God, you are exalted and cannot suffer, but in your body, in which all your souls are in harmony, you are not fully exalted or beyond anguish. Lord, you therefore have the same yearning and aspiration that you endured on your cross. Lord, all this dwelt within you from the very beginning. Lord, you will have this devotional yearning and aspiration until the last soul to be redeemed has been brought into your exaltation.

Lord God, you have the combined virtues of unfathomable care and tenderness, with aspiration and yearning. (Through this virtue of yearning within you Lord, we in turn yearn for you: Lord you have shown that without it no soul shall be redeemed and enter heaven.) This distinction of aspiration and yearning come from God's infinite devotion, just as tenderness does. Though aspiration and tenderness are at variance, devotional yearning comes from them both together. It is an unfathomable yearning, which carries on as long as we have temporal longings, bringing us forth into your infinite exaltation.

Lord, through all this you have shown in your enlightenment and devotion, your unfathomable care and tenderness, that you will not permit Judgement Day to come until the perfect hour. Amen.

THE THIRTEENTH REVELATION

CHAPTER 32

How all things will be agreeable and all manner of things will be agreeable.

Lord Jesus Christ, you have shown that all things will be agreeable; and that all manner of things will be agreeable.

Lord, you want us to discern that you have consideration not only for the eminent and considerable things but also of the insignificant and minute, trifling and uncomplicated things- all are equivalent, nothing will be omitted.

Lord, in our finite mortal minds, when we consider the iniquity that we behold as so vile and that creates so much anguish, it appears inconceivable that anything agreeable could evolve from them. We cannot abide in your bliss of considering God, as we should, as we are engrossed in this iniquity and anguish and have regrets. Our temporal minds are so without vision, so lowly, and so unwise, that we don't perceive the exalted and awesome enlightenment, the dominion and the benevolence of the divine Trinity. Lord Jesus, you have shown that you want us only to dwell on the fact, with conviction and confidence, that you will make all things agreeable. Lord, you want us to discern it now before we behold it fully in bliss on Judgement Day.

Lord, you want to give us reassurance by considering all the acts that God has planned. All the living souls on earth cannot know how and when the last act of the divine Trinity will take place. You have shown Lord, that God wants us only to concern ourselves with the fact that it will take place. We should, therefore, be less distressed and be serene in our devotion, by not dwelling on all the distressing things that prevent us from totally having bliss in him.

Lord, you have shown that this immense act, decreed by our Lord God in the beginning, cherished and concealed within his divine domain, discerned only by himself, through which he will make all things agreeable.

Lord, the divine Trinity made all things from nought, so the divine Trinity will make all things agreeable, that are not.

Lord God, you have shown through our belief that you will keep your promises in every aspect. Just as there are souls that are going to be redeemed, so there are souls that are going to be condemned. Lord, you have shown angels have come down from heaven as a result of their vainglory and are now demons. Mortals who die outside the belief of Holy Church will be excluded from God's devotion. Anybody who is baptised but lives an unchristian mortal existence will be excluded from God's devotion; they will be condemned to hell for infinity.

Lord God, you have shown that you want us to discern that what may appear inconceivable to us is not inconceivable to you. Lord, you have shown that you will keep your promises in every aspect, and that all things will be agreeable. Lord, through your benevolence you want us to hold fast to this conviction.

Lord God, you have shown that this is the immense act that you will accomplish, when this occurs you will keep your promise and make everything that is not well, agreeable. Amen.

THE THIRTEENTH REVELATION

CHAPTER 33

How it is God's desire that we give immense consideration to all the acts that he has achieved, but not to be engrossed in concern on what his last act will be.

Lord God, Heavenly Father, you have shown that you and all the divine company of heaven, do not debate the devil or any living soul, who is the same condition as the devil in this temporal life and at death- even if that person has been baptised.

Lord God, you desire to encourage us and to teach us to adhere to every detail of our belief.

Lord, it is your desire that we give immense concern to all the acts that you have achieved, but not to be engrossed in concern on what your last act will be. May we aspire to be as the divine company of heaven is, who desire nothing but your will, Lord? They are totally contented whether you conceal or impart to them. Lord, you have shown that you wish us to discern that the more we concern ourselves to know your concealed enigmas, concerning this or any other issue, the greater will be the concealment of the reality to us. Amen.

THE THIRTEENTH REVELATION

CHAPTER 34

How our benevolent Lord will most compassionately reveal to us the entirety that is needful for us to grasp and discern.

Lord God, Heavenly Father, you have shown that you desire us to discern that there are two sorts of enigmas. One is the immense enigma and the many aspects associated with it, that you desire us to acknowledge that are concealed until you proclaim them bountifully. The other enigmas are those that you wish us to discern now, undoubtedly. These appear more of an enigma to us, as we are so without vision and unenlightened. Lord, you have shown that you have immense compassion on us and accordingly you will make them more perceptible for us, so that we may discern you, have devotion for you and embrace you. Lord, through your discernment and the oration and enlightenment of Holy Church, you have shown that you will tenderly bestow the entirety to us that is required for us to determine and perceive.

Lord God, you have immense rapture in the souls who devotedly and meekly acknowledge the oration and enlightenment of Holy Church. Lord, the Holy Church is your domain, your entity, your enlightenment; you are the guide, the consummation, and the honour for which every living soul aspires to. This is discerned now and shall be discerned to every living soul to whom the Holy Spirit pronounces it.

Lord, all that you have discerned should encourage us to thwart iniquity. For Lord, you have shown that you undertake the entirety that is accomplished without any iniquity, and that all will be agreeable. And Lord, when you do bestow that there is iniquity, you desire us to discern that all will be agreeable. Amen.

THE THIRTEENTH REVELATION

CHAPTER 35

How God performs all that is benevolent, and embraces all righteousness and tolerates iniquity through his compassionate and benevolent undertaking.

Lord God, Heavenly Father, you have shown that it brings more exaltation to you if we examine entity collectively rather than to have bliss in one particular aspect. If we conduct ourselves with this enlightenment according to your discernment, then nought will make us particularly blissful, but nought will make us wretched, as all will be agreeable. Lord, you have shown that you want us to discern that our complete bliss derives from beholding you in entity. Just as you created entity through your divine dominion, enlightenment and devotion, so you will continually guide entity to the equivalent consummation. Lord, you have shown that you yourself will convey entity to its culmination, and we shall behold it in the perfect hour.

Lord, you have shown that the entity that you bestow is righteous, and the entity you empower bestows exaltation to you. This embraces all righteousness and iniquity, for the entity that is righteous you bestow and the entity that is iniquitous you tolerate. Lord, by tolerating iniquity you desire us to discern that iniquity is not honourable, but by tolerating it you bring exaltation to yourself. Lord, through this toleration, as we bestow your compassion and benevolence at your undertaking, we discern more of your righteousness, which is imparted with such wonderful lowliness and compassion.

An aspect is righteous when it is so honourable that it cannot be excelled. Lord, you are pure righteousness and all your undertakings are bestowed honourably, as you decreed from infinity in your sovereign domain, enlightenment and benevolence. In righteousness you decreed entity for perfection and in righteousness you always undertake, guiding entity to the equal consummation, and you always have complete bliss in all your undertakings. Through your benevolence it is infinitely delightful for the soul that beholds this divine accord. Lord, you have shown that through your benevolence you infinitely elect that all souls in the company of heaven are beheld as infinitely righteous by you, and higher than all living things you remarkably enfold us secure in righteousness.

Lord, you have shown that compassion is an undertaking that derives from your benevolence, and the undertaking of compassion will endure as long as iniquity is tolerated tormenting righteous souls. When iniquity is no longer tolerated, then the undertaking of compassion will be consummated. The entity will be brought into righteousness for eternity. Lord, you tolerate us descending into iniquity; but through your delightful devotion, your domain and enlightenment we are kept secure, and by your forgiveness and benevolence we are elevated to manifold immense exaltations.

Lord, with devotion you desire us to discern you in eternity on account of your righteousness and forgiveness. May we be the souls that by benevolent enlightenment behold this and have bliss with both, and have exaltation for eternity? Amen.

THE THIRTEENTH REVELATION

CHAPTER 36

Of another exalted undertaking of our Lord, which, by blessing, may be discerned to a degree here. How we should have bliss in the same, and how our God still performs miracles.

Lord God, Heavenly Father, you have shown that you yourself will carry out an act on earth. Our iniquity will not hinder your benevolence from being achieved. Lord, if we revere you and desire only to do what you ordain, through your benevolence we may behold with bliss, that iniquity will not prevent you carrying out this act.

This act begun on earth will bring exaltation to you and immense benevolence to your devoted on earth. This shall continue until the perfect hour and we shall discern it as we ascend to our divine abode. Its exaltation and delight shall continue for infinity before you, Lord, and all the divine company of heaven.

Lord, you have shown that this act will have immense importance, and in this knowledge you desire us to have delight in you and all your undertakings. Although this important act will be an enigma to us, we should accept with devotion and conviction, that it will come to pass.

Lord, in this way you have shown that you desire us to have no dread of the things you discern us to behold. You behold them, that through the discernment we might have devotion for you, have bliss in you, and have exaltation in you for infinity. Lord, it is out of your immense devotion for us that you behold the entity that is elevated and for our benevolence at that juncture. It is also out of your immense benevolence that you behold to us that the enigmas are concealed from us, equally desiring for us to discern that we shall behold them in our infinite delight. So now we should have jubilation, not only for what we behold, but also for the enigmas.

Lord, you desire for us to discern that this is for all the souls that will be redeemed. You yourself, shall eminently, incredibly, bountifully accomplish your word. Although your living souls commit iniquity- it will be the most immense delight to behold the act that you yourself will accomplish.

Lord, you desire us to behold that through this discernment there are elements for meekness, for devotion, for self-denial. Here is delight in you. Because of your devotion for us in entity, we should delight in you, giving you the most immense bliss.

Lord, in our temporal lives, at times when in our folly we veer to what is denounced, you compassionately inspire us. In our immense bliss you arouse the souls of your beloved children, by imparting that we should depart from what we have become devoted to. You teach us that we should discern that we should veer to you, that you are our entity, that in you, our Saviour and redeemer we shall find our delight.

Lord, it is your undertaking, through benevolence for our souls, for us to have perception to behold and experience this.

Lord, you have shown this act will occur to each soul as it ascends into heaven. You may behold it to some souls on earth.

Lord, you have imparted a significant discernment of the undertaking of miracles. You have imparted that you have accomplished various miracles throughout history- miracles that are encouraging, awesome, divine and immense. What you have accomplished, you still impart, and you shall always impart in the future.

Lord, you have shown to us that our affliction, distress and immense torment descend upon us before a miracle occurs. These take place so that we may discern our own fragility and the suffering our iniquity creates for us, and then meekly revere you Lord, with awe, as we beseech you for forgiveness and benevolence. Following this, Lord, miracles are imparted from your sovereign domain, enlightenment and benevolence. As far as it is conceivable in this fleeting temporal life they discern to us Lord, your righteousness and the bliss of heaven, in order to encourage us in our belief, giving anticipation in benevolence. Lord, you have delight when we discern you and revere you through miracles.

Lord, you have shown that it is not your desire that we are burdened by the difficulties and strife that descends on us, for it shall always be in this manner before a miracle occurs. Amen.

THE THIRTEENTH REVELATION

CHAPTER 37

How in all that are going to be redeemed there is a divine will that has never yielded to iniquity, and never shall. Our distress originates because our own benevolence is imperfect.

Lord God, Heavenly Father, you have shown that every living soul will have iniquity in their temporal life. You desire us to discern that this iniquity should not cause any anxiety to develop in us. You have promised that you will keep us very protected. Lord, you have shown through your benevolent word, that you will keep this pledge of divine guardianship, which is more immense than we will ever be able to discern in our temporal life. For just as all souls will have iniquity in their life, all companions in Christ will be provided with a balance of encouragement, sanctuary and guardianship.

Lord, you have shown that you have devotion for all that are companions in Christ, who are going to be redeemed, as though one person.

Lord, you desire us to discern that in all living souls

there is a debased side of character that cannot desire what is benevolent. But there is also a divine desire, which has never given consent to iniquity, or will ever do so for infinity. This divine desire is our elevated character, which is so devout that it cannot desire what is iniquitous, but only what is benevolent. Through this Lord, you have devotion for us and we can give you rapture for infinity.

Lord, you have shown how you behold us and enfold us in your absolute devotion. Undoubtedly, your devotion for us is as immense for us in our temporal life, as it will be when we behold you in your sovereign domain. All our tribulations are created through our own imperfect devotion. Amen.

THE THIRTEENTH REVELATION

CHAPTER 38

Examples of how the impressions of iniquity shall be altered to exaltation.

Lord God, Heavenly Father, you have additionally shown that iniquity will not culminate in dishonour, but exaltation. Reality necessitates that every iniquity be bestowed its equivalent anguish, so devotion imparts to the equal soul a benediction for every iniquity. Appropriately, as manifold iniquities are chastised with manifold anguishes corresponding to their gravity, so in heaven they will be honoured with manifold raptures corresponding to the anguish and grief they imparted to the souls' temporal existence. Lord, the soul that ascends into heaven is inestimable to you, and its position in heaven is so honoured that your benevolence will never consent to a redeemed soul to descend into iniquity without compensating that soul for the iniquity. Lord, in your sovereign domain you will bestow the discernment for infinity that the soul is renewed to entire rapture by your sovereign exaltation.

Lord, you have shown that you desire us to commemorate the innumerable saints from the Old Testament and those from the New Testament. You desire us to bear in mind that they were also iniquitous in their temporal life- and the temporal Church discerns it- however, they were not dishonoured but instead it has come about that they are exalted in your sovereign domain. Lord, through your tenderness you let us behold something in our temporal life of what we shall completely discern in your sovereign domain. For in your sovereign abode of heaven the stain of iniquity is converted to exaltation. Amen.

THE THIRTEENTH REVELATION

CHAPTER 39

How iniquity is the harshest scourge, by remorse we are made faultless; by mercy we are prepared; by genuine yearning for God we are made worthy for him.

Lord God, Heavenly Father, you have shown that iniquity is the harshest scourge with which your elected living souls can be chastised with. It is an affliction that torments both men and women, making them abhor themselves so much they think that you will condemn them to hell. But Lord, through your benevolence you caress us through the Holy Spirit until we are furnished with penitence and our hostility is converted into confidence of your benevolent forgiveness. Then Lord, you commence to restore our anguish and awaken our souls as we veer to the entity of Holy Church.

Lord, you have shown that through your devoted benevolence the Holy Spirit guides us to eagerly, plainly and sincerely acknowledge our iniquities. As we have dishonoured your adorable concept we are furnished with immense regret and contempt. Lord, you teach through the Holy Spirit and the Holy Church that we should have a deed of atonement for our iniquities, which is a deed of lowliness and which gives you immense rapture. Lord, you have shown that we should consent to any mortal infirmity that you impart to us, in unison with anguish and indignities, and the disapproval and disdain of this world, and all manner of tribulation and enticements, either divine or temporal, into which we find ourselves descending.

Lord, through your most compassionate devotion, you enfold us at the moment when we believe, that because of our iniquity, we might be abandoned and thrust off. Through this and your benevolence we discern lowliness, as a result we are ascended up eminently in your beholding, and we discern an immense remorse, tenderness and pure yearning for you. Then we are unexpectedly ransomed from iniquity and anguish and elevated to rapture and are alike the divine company of your heavenly domain.

Lord, you have shown that by remorse we are made pure; by tenderness we are made ready; by devoted yearning we are made deserving of you. Lord, you desire the transgressors in their temporal life who are going to be redeemed to discern that these are the three phases that a soul can enter into your heavenly domain. These remedies must restore every transgressor. You restore us Lord, but you still behold our torments. You transcend the torments into awards. Entity is transformed and overturned. In our temporal lives we are chastised with remorse and atonement, in our heavenly abode we shall be given honour by your forbearing devotion. Lord, you do not wish to strip any redeemed soul, who enters your divine domain, of the most insignificant blessing achieved from their conflicts. Lord, through your devotion for us you behold iniquity as anguish and torment for your devoted and you do not condemn us. As the honour imparted will be immense, illustrious and exalted, so disgrace will be transformed to devotion and more rapture.

Lord, through your compassion you have shown that you desire your devoted souls not to be despondent because they descend so frequently and so harshly into iniquity. Lord, our descending into iniquity does not impede your devotion for us.

We may not always be in a condition of harmony and devotion, but these are always spirited and vibrant inside us. Lord, you desire us to discern that through your devotion you are the bedrock of the entity of our existence, and furthermore, that you are our infinite guardian. With your entire immense domain you enfold us from our foes that assail us so ruthlessly and maliciously- and our distress is decidedly immense because we impart so many occasions by our weaknesses. Amen.

THE THIRTEENTH REVELATION

CHAPTER 40

How genuine benevolence imparts discernment that for love's consideration only we should abhor iniquity. God revealed that there is no more grievous hell than iniquity. We must forever abhor iniquity and forever have benevolence for the higher entity as God has.

Lord God, Heavenly Father, you have shown a sign of your incomparable affection by keeping us so gently folded while we were in iniquity. You also manifest our iniquity to us with a very profound effect in the cherished radiance of your compassion and benevolence. When we discern how abominable we are we presume you will be wrathful with us for our iniquity. But through the Holy Spirit we are inspired to pray in penitence and to yearn with all our strength to amend our temporal lives and appease your wrath until we are able to consummate tranquillity of soul and a calm sense of right and wrong. Then we long that you have given us remission for our iniquity- and you assuredly have. Lord, you then compassionately and enthusiastically impart yourself to our souls, with a delighted manifestation and an affectionate acceptance. It is as though our soul has come out of confinement and anguish and that you discern your delight that we have veered to you, and you impart that you were beside us throughout our anguish and that we can behold your devotion and be unified in bliss.

Lord, through this our souls benevolently encounter the compassionate operation of the Holy Spirit, and the righteousness of Christ's Holy Passion, and our iniquities are redeemed in blessing and forbearance. Our souls are received with bliss and exaltation, as when they ascend into heaven.

Lord, you have shown that in your immense benevolence you have created much for us, to the extent that when we abide in tranquillity and devotion we shall truly be redeemed. We cannot fully discern this in our temporal life; we should always aspire to abide with our Lord Jesus in affectionate prayer and devoted yearning. Lord Jesus, you have shown that you have divine yearning to bear us into complete bliss.

Lord, through all this divine inspiration we should not behold iniquity heedlessly. We should discern with true devotion, that true love alone should make us abhor iniquity. Lord, the more that every temporal devoted soul discerns this in your meek devoted graciousness, the more immense will be the abhorrence of iniquity, and the appreciation of dishonour.

Lord, you have shown that there is no more immense hell than iniquity for the devoted soul. For if we could discern before us all the anguish there is in hell and in purgatory and on earth and discern iniquity on its own, we would desire anguish rather than iniquity. For iniquity is so evil and so completely abhorrent.

Lord, when we pledge ourselves to devotion and

lowliness you benevolently and compassionately renew our gracefulness and purity. You are as desirous to redeem us as you are enlightened and mightily capable to redeem us. Lord Jesus, you yourself are the foundation of all the laws of Christian men. Lord, you taught us to be benevolent in answer to iniquity. We can discern that you are this devotion, and you impart what you discern us to do. You desire us to resemble you in dedicated boundless devotion, towards our fellow companions and us. You never part from us with your devotion because of our iniquity, so you desire us not to part our devotion from ourselves or from our fellow companions. We should always abhor iniquity and be forever devoted to the soul as our Lord God is. Lord, our eternal inspiration is that you shall keep us enfolded in your care. Amen.

THE FOURTEENTH REVELATION

CHAPTER 41

The Fourteenth Revelation shows how our Lord God is the domain of our prayer: he entreats us to pray and imparts all that is essential.

Lord God, Heavenly Father, you have given us discernment regarding prayer. You have shown that there are two conditions of prayer: one is righteousness and the other pure belief.

Our frailty in prayer is when we do not fully believe that we are devoted enough for you to hear us Lord. Consequently we are frequently as empty and thirsty after praying as we were before.

Lord, you have shown that you are the domain of our prayer. It is your desire that we have something, then you make that our desire too; then you make us implore you for it- and we do implore you for it.

Lord, you give us immense inspiration by showing that when we implore you this imparts immense bliss to you and you shall impart honour for infinity for our praying. You show us that when we implore you we shall always have your forgiveness and benevolence. You make us implore you for the entity that you ordained from infinity. You desire your devoted souls on earth to comprehend as much as possible that you are the domain for our prayer, and thereby we should pray more.

Lord God, imploring you in prayer is a pure abiding undertaking of desire, accomplished in devotion by the soul, which is in union and turned to your desire, by the beloved central undertaking of the Holy Spirit.

Lord, you have shown that you are the first person to encounter our prayer with appreciation and bliss. You elevate them to your cherished abode where they will never expire. With the company of heaven you consent to our prayer, and it dwells everlastingly in your presence, constantly advancing our purpose. When we ascend in your heavenly domain you shall impart it to us with greater bliss, with your infinite appreciation and exaltation.

Lord, you have shown that our prayers make you immensely delighted and blissful. You require and desire them, as it is your holy desire to fashion us, through your benevolence, as allied to you in the manner of our perceptions as we are allied to you in our central character. Lord, you desire that we devoutly pray from deep down, even when we have no inclination, perception, beholding or belief that we can accomplish it, for it is beneficial to us. For in those arid, barren, feeble and low times our prayer is immensely agreeable to you, even if we discern that it has contributed negligibly to our temporal life. This is right for all our faithful prayer.

Lord, you desire us to constantly pray in your presence so that you may infinitely impart your appreciation. Despite our own perceptions you consent to our devoted purposes. You have bliss in our endeavours to pray and to living a devout life, through your aid and benevolence, enlightening and delicately controlling all our reason to you, until in absolute bliss we are blessed with the one we wish to behold, Jesus.

Lord, you have also shown that appreciation is also essential to prayer. Appreciation is a pure inmost enlightenment; with bountiful adoration and devoted awe you guide us to veer with all our fortitude to the undertaking you are entreating us to accomplish, all the time delighting and appreciating you in our emotions. Occasionally it pours out in speech as we show appreciation and give you exaltation. Occasionally when our emotions are arid and we perceive nothing, or when Satan is attacking, comprehension and benevolence compel us to exclaim outwardly to you, as we remember Jesus' Holy Passion and immense benevolence. Then Lord, through your dominion your word is imparted to the soul, delivering entity to our emotions, guiding us through your benevolence into the pure undertaking for you, fashioning our soul to pray with complete bliss. Lord, you behold that the most blissful appreciation we can impart to you is to delight in you. Amen.

THE FOURTEENTH REVELATION

CHAPTER 42

For prayer with immense yearning and complete faith convey a virtuous discernment of the abundance of bliss that is to occur.

Lord God, Heavenly Father, you have shown that you desire that we have complete discernment regarding prayer. Lord, you are the foundation of our prayers through your benevolence and your desire. You desire that our determination should be in union with your purpose with immense bliss. Through this union we should resemble you in entirety. Lord, you have shown that you will aid us and in unison we shall accomplish it as you have decreed. We worship you!

Lord, it is your desire that our prayer and our faith are immense. If our faith is not as immense as our praying, we do not completely glorify you Lord. We restrict and impair ourselves when we do not fully discern that you Lord are the foundation of our prayer, bestowing our prayer to us through your devotion and benevolence. If we fully discerned this we would be able to have faith that we have all we long for as an offering from you Lord. We can be sure that if we pray to you Lord with conviction for pardon and benevolence, you shall firstly give your compassion and benevolence to us.

Lord, you have shown that occasionally we may have the impression that we have prayed for a prolonged time, with no result, but you desire us not to be disheartened. We should hold on for a more suitable time, or for greater benevolence, or a finer offering. Lord, you desire for us to discern in truth that you are Being itself and to have the foundation of our discernment in this enlightenment with all the intensity, conviction and principle that we are blessed with. Lord, it is your desire that on this foundation we should come to rest and make our abode. Lord, you also desire that we should discern the following in the enlightenment of your benevolence that you bestow upon us. First our supreme formation; second our inestimable and priceless salvation; third that you have formed all lower things to be of use to us and you maintain them out of your devotion for us.

Lord, you desire us to discern that before we began praying all the exalted acts have already been accomplished, as the Holy Church teaches. We should thankfully behold this and be praying for what you are now accomplishing Lord, so that you may command and direct us in our temporal life to your exaltation and ascend us into your rapture.

Lord, you have shown that we should equally discern

that you are accomplishing this, and pray for it. One is insufficient. Lord, if we pray and do not have enlightenment that you are accomplishing things we become dispirited and uncertain, and that does not bestow exaltation to you. Also if we discern your accomplishments and do not pray, we are not bestowing what is due to you Lord. If we discern your accomplishments and pray for your acts- that is how we give you exaltation and encourage ourselves. Lord, it is your desire that we pray for the entirety that you have ordained to complete both particularly and extensively. The exaltation and rapture that this bestows to you Lord and the appreciation and devotion that you shall bestow to us far exceeds our discernment.

Lord, this prayer with immense aspiration and total faith bestows a correct discernment of the complete exaltation that will be accomplished. The yearning comes when we are unsuccessful in accomplishing the divine exaltation that by character we are ordained for; faith comes through benevolence, as we develop in complete discernment and love, and affectionately contemplate our Saviour. Lord, you everlastingly observe whether we are occupied in these two acts, for it is our role- and in your benevolence Lord you cannot bestow anything inferior.

Lord, we should give our utmost even though we shall discern that it is of no consequence. But if we achieve all we can and pray earnestly for redemption and benevolence, then whatever is our shortcoming we shall ascertain in you Lord. This is what you wish us to discern that you are the foundation of our praying. Through this you have shown the complete conquest that is bestowed over all our imperfections and all our distrustful apprehension. Amen.

THE FOURTEENTH REVELATION

CHAPTER 43

Prayer unites our higher entity to God.

Lord God, Heavenly Father, you have shown that prayer joins the soul to you. Through your grace our soul is renewed to be similar to your character, although it is frequently unlike your character through our iniquity. Through prayer our soul aspires to your aspirations Lord, it inspires our moral sense and allows us to be bestowed with your benevolence. You enlighten us to pray and have total belief that you shall bestow our earthly longings. You behold us in benevolence and desire that we are joined in your devoted acts; you inspire us to pray for what gives you rapture to ordain. You reciprocate that prayer and our devoted aspirations with an offering of everlasting honour.

Lord, you have shown this through our petitions to you. Through our petitions you have shown that you have immense rapture, as if you owed us for our devotion, when it is you who imparts all devoted benevolence, we only earnestly implore you to do what is benevolent. Nothing could give you greater rapture than for us to implore you earnestly, discerningly and solemnly to ordain your will. Through this our soul develops in conformity with you Lord God.

Lord, when you kindly show yourself to our souls, then we have what we long for and for a time we do not discern that there could be more to pray for. Then our whole entity is fixed on beholding you. This prayer is incomparable and immeasurable; we should be in union with you Lord and engrossed in the discernment and consideration of you. For a time we will be able to pray for nothing but what you inspire us to pray for. This we do with immense rapture and devoted awe, with an enlightenment of affection and bliss in you. The more a soul discerns you Lord, the more it longs for you through your benevolence.

Lord, when we do not discern you then our frustration implores us to pray to Jesus for guidance. When our souls are stricken and reviled and remain abandoned in wretchedness, then we should pray that our soul may become receptive and yielding to you Lord. You have shown that you will always be perceptive to our souls in your devotion Lord.

Lord, you have shown that you guide us in our longing to pray, encouraging us in our aspirations. Through a particular benevolence when we discern you distinctly apart, then we pursue your guidance and through your devotion you bring us forth to yourself. You have shown that all our gifts and proficiency are suffused with your wondrous and bountiful benevolence. Lord, you are constantly imparting your acts in many spheres, and your ordination is so gracious, so enlightened and so sovereign that it immensely exceeds all temporal creativity and resourcefulness and contemplation. All there is then is to behold you in rapture, earnestly aspiring to be in total unison to you, to make your heavenly abode our home, to rejoice in your benevolence and appreciate your devotion.

Lord, through our meek continuous prayer we shall be in union with you, we shall discern you through your numerous cherished contacts, that impart affectionate spiritual enlightenment and perception, in accordance with what our natural character can behold. This is imparted through the benevolence of the Holy Spirit for all our temporal life, furnished with aspiration for your devotion. When our temporal life ends we shall completely discern ourselves and devotedly be blessed with you Lord. Then we shall be enfolded by you Lord, discerning you completely, perceiving you entirely, ascertain you divinely, in your delightful aroma and savouring your affection.

Lord, we shall discern your countenance with our face, affably and entirely. Your creation will infinitely discern and behold his God. We cannot discern you in this way in our temporal life and go on living. But Lord, through your particular benevolence when you ordain to impart yourself in our temporal life, you intensify your creation above its capacity, measuring your manifestation in accordance with your ordination and in the most valuable direction. Amen.

44-63. These are contemplation about the previous Fourteen Revelations.

CHAPTER 44

How God is infinite exalted validity, enlightenment and benevolence. God who is the uncreated has created man, bestowing his attributes to the higher entity of man.

Lord God, Heavenly Father, you have previously shown that your creation is constantly striving to carry out your aspirations and exaltation.

Genuineness discerns you Lord and enlightenment contemplates on you. Flowing from these is devotion, which is a divine, awesome rapture in you Lord. Where genuineness and enlightenment sincerely exist, devotion is also in existence from these. This is your ordination Lord, for you are infinite absolute genuineness, infinite absolute enlightenment and infinite absolute devotion. Lord God, you who were uncreated have created man; bestowing your attributes to our soul. Our soul was made to contemplate and be devoted to you Lord. So Lord, you have rapture in your creation, and your creation has infinite overflowing bliss.

Lord, in our contemplation we discern you, our maker, so exalted, so illustrious, so benevolent that in contrast your creation appears almost nothing. However, the radiance and purity of genuineness and enlightenment make us behold and discern that we were created for devotion, and in this devotion you keep us for infinity Lord. Amen.

CHAPTER 45

Of the immense wisdom of God, and the alternating wisdom of men.

Lord God, Heavenly Father, you have shown that the foundation of your discernment of us in your benevolence is on our higher nature; which is complete and united with you. Our own discernment varies and very often fails because sometimes it is affected by our higher nature and sometimes by our lower nature. Consequently, it can either be benevolent and accepting or ruthless and grievous. If our discernment is benevolent and accepting it is of your integrity Lord. Where our discernment is ruthless and grievous, Lord Jesus Christ, you reform it by the dominion of your holy Passion, and therefore make it harmonise to your pure discernment.

Lord, you have shown that the two judgements are harmonised and joined together, but each one will be acknowledged individually in your heavenly abode.

Lord, you created the benevolent and accepting judgement in our higher nature by putting your sovereign, infinite entity there. Through this kind, affectionate discernment you attribute no fault to us.

Lord, the entity of your heavenly abode and the entity of our temporal abode encompasses the two judgements. The greater that our aspiration is by the benevolence of the Holy Spirit to differentiate and comprehend them, the more we shall behold and discern our imperfections and, by your benevolence Lord, the more immense will be our instinctive yearning to overflow with infinite exaltation and rapture. Lord, this was the purpose of our creation that our higher nature is overflowing with your rapture, and shall be for infinity. Amen.

CHAPTER 46

How in our lower entity we must discern ourselves iniquitous. But God is never wrathful, but he is a close guardian to our higher entity.

Lord God, Heavenly Father, you have shown that in our transitory life here, our temporal character does not discern what our true character is. When we genuinely and distinctly behold and discern our real character then we shall genuinely and distinctly behold and discern you Lord, in absolute exaltation. The nearer that we are Lord to this complete exaltation, the more immense shall be our yearning in our character and for your benevolence. We may come to discern our genuine character in our temporal life through the persistent aid and domain of our higher nature and our enlightenment may aspire to greater heights with the aid of blessing and benevolence. We shall, however, never completely discern our genuine character until the end of our temporal life Lord. It is righteous that spontaneously and by benevolence we should devoutly yearn for and wish to discern our true character in complete and infinite rapture.

Lord, we can discern that you give us constant, infinite devotion with absolute sanctuary and the assurance of rapturous redemption. We should also have devotion and revere the enlightenment that Holy Church gives us to acknowledge and admit that we are iniquitous in our acts. We do not discharge all benevolent acts that we could, and as a result we should have your anguish and wrath Lord.

Regardless of this, however, Lord you have shown that you are not wrathful, for as our Lord God, Heavenly Father, you are benevolence, entity, genuineness, devotion and tranquillity. Your virtue and righteousness do not permit you to be wrathful. You have shown that wrath is adverse to the character of your domain, your enlightenment and your benevolence. Our soul is in unison with you Lord, amidst you and our soul, you do not behold wrath or the necessity for absolution. This is because Lord you have shown that in your benevolence you have so absolutely affiliated our soul to you, that all entity cannot separate us.

Lord, you have shown that it is your desire for us to learn this, as far as your temporal creatures can discern such entity. All that our elementary souls can discern you desire to impart to us Lord. In your devotion, however, Lord with vigour and enlightenment you do not impart the enigmas to us. We shall never discern these enigmas until through your benevolence Lord, you have made us capable to behold them. We should be reconciled to bide our time till you impart your ordination in these sovereign enigmas Lord. Amen.

CHAPTER 47

How through our iniquity we have a lack of vision and do not behold God. We descend into the regression of our narrow depraved entity.

Lord God, Heavenly Father, you have shown that our soul has a calling to meditate devoutly and agonise patiently. Lord, you desire us to discern that we shall soon behold distinctly all that we long to understand.

Lord, you have shown some of your ordination of the undertaking of benevolence. In our temporal life we are so wavering. As a consequence of our weakness we descend into iniquity and we are overwhelmed. We are fragile and unwise and our resolution is readily conquered. In our temporal life we endure turmoil, tribulation and remorse because we are without vision and do not behold you Lord. If we were to persistently behold you Lord, we would have no base emotions or any of the inclinations or desires that minister to iniquity.

Lord, you have shown that there can be five undertakings for our souls in the temporal life: exaltation, remorse, yearning, apprehension, and assured anticipation. Exaltation, because you have shown Lord that we can behold you. Our remorse is because of our weakness. Yearning that we may behold you more and more immensely Lord, while discerning that we shall never completely be at peace until we behold you fully and distinctly in your heavenly abode. Apprehension, because it appears we may be abandoned. Assured anticipation, in your infinite devotion, in which we shall be enfolded by your benevolence and ascended into your exaltation.

Lord, we should have such bliss in the assured anticipation of your benevolent guardianship, giving us solace so that the remorse and apprehension of our temporal life are not as grievous as they could be. You have shown Lord that we cannot constantly behold you in this way in our temporal life, but when it declines it is for your exaltation that we may have more immense, infinite bliss. As a consequence we frequently do not behold you and descend into the regression of our own entity. Here there is no vestige of anything that is honourable but only narrow depravity, which has developed from the original foundation of our iniquity, and from all the other iniquities of our own creation. As a consequence we are oppressed and disturbed with the enlightenment of iniquity and the numerous forms of anguish both devotional and incarnate, which we are so acquainted with in our temporal life. Amen.

CHAPTER 48

Of the attributes of mercy and grace: both undertake differently but are established in equal benevolence.

Our benevolent Lord, the Holy Spirit, you who are eternal entity abide in our soul, keeping us protected. Through your benevolence you undertake throughout us, bestowing repose and tranquillity, unity with you and reverence. Lord, this is your forgiveness and your way of persistently guiding us throughout the fluctuations in our temporal life.

Lord, you have shown that the only wrath is in us and you have absolved us of that. Our own wrath is a contrary hostility to serenity and devotion. It originates from our absence of dominion, or absence of enlightenment, or absence of benevolence- the absence is not in you Lord, but in us. Our baseness and iniquity are deplorably and constantly conflicting with tranquillity and devotion. Lord, you show this in your benevolent manifestation of mercy and compassion. The foundation of forgiveness is devotion, and it is forgiveness' undertaking to enfold us securely in devotion. Lord, you have shown that forgiveness and devotion cannot be parted.

Lord, your forgiveness is an affectionate, compassionate, devoted undertaking, overflowing with tenderness. Forgiveness undertakes throughout us, enfolding us, bestowing everything that results in advantage for us. Forgiveness through devotion imparts in us a measure of shortcoming, and the measure of our shortcoming is the measure of our decline, and the measure of our decline is the measure of our expiring. We are destined to expire if we do not keep our vision and perception of you Lord, who is eternal entity. Our shortcoming is grievous, our declining base, our expiring piteous. But Lord, your affectionate contemplation of compassion and devotion never moves apart from us, and the undertaking of your forgiveness never comes to naught.

Lord, you have shown that the aspect of forgiveness and benevolence are both undertaken differently, but have their foundation in the equivalent devotion. Your forgiveness is understanding- it is shown in the delicate devotion of a mother; benevolence is illustrious- it is shown in a regal leader who commands with the same devotion.

Lord, your forgiveness is functioning: it gives sanctuary, it adopts us, renews us, and cures us, imparted in entire affectionate devotion.

Lord, your benevolence is also functioning. It elevates and honours us, constantly eclipsing anything our desires and undertakings could merit and outwardly manifests your principal majestic dominion and your awesome affection; imparted from your bountiful devotion. Your benevolence converts our appalling shortcoming into abundant and continuous solace; our base decline into exalted recovery and our piteous expiring into righteous, sacred entity.

Lord, you have shown that as our intransigence ends in anguish, dishonour and regret in our temporal life, your benevolence imparts a more immense degree of your heavenly abode's solace, exaltation and rapture. This is to the extent that when we are imparted with your affectionate honour that your benevolence has secured for us, we shall show our gratitude and glorify you, continually delighting that we prevailed through affliction. It is an element of this divine devotion Lord that we shall discern in you that we have enlightenment that we would never have been imparted with if we had not first endured affliction. We should admit Lord that it is our wrath that is hushed and banished by your compassion and forgiveness. Amen.

CHAPTER 49

How peace has dominion where our Lord has sovereignty and wrath cannot exist. Our higher entity is genuinely serene when it is unified to God.

Lord God, Heavenly Father, you have shown that it is inconceivable for you to be wrathful. Lord, you have shown that the foundation and entrenchment of our complete entity is in devotion and without devotion we would expire. You impart your exceptional benevolence to souls so that they are empowered to discern your exalted and miraculous mercy, and to behold that we are everlastingly unified to you in devotion, and to such a soul it is inconceivable that you could be wrathful. Wrath and benevolence are incompatible. Lord, through your benevolence, meekness and compassion you banish and extinguish our wrath, so that we grow to become devoted, lowly and compassionate. This is contrary to wrath.

Lord, you have distinctly shown that serenity has ordinance in your dominion, and wrath has no position. Lord, there is no form of wrath in you momentary or enduring, for if you were wrathful to us for a moment we would expire. Lord, your power, enlightenment and infinite benevolence created our entity, so you enfold us through this. We are aware of our baseness, our overflowing of conflict and strife, however we are enclosed by your compassion and meekness, affection and benevolence. Lord, it is your desire for us to behold that our infinite harmony, our abode, our entity and our existence are in you.

Lord, the infinite benevolence that enfolds us when we are iniquitous so that we do not expire persistently imparts harmony instead of our wrath and our defiant retreat. This imparts in us an earnest dread and we behold our shortcoming so that gravely we entreat you for your mercy, desiring your benevolence, for our redemption.

Lord, although our lack of vision and frailty has empowered the wrath and defiance within us to steer us into torment, anguish and affliction, you entirely enfold us in your compassion, so that we do not expire. But we shall not be rapturously secure, with the infinite bliss of your abode Lord, until we are overflowing with harmony and devotion. Then Lord, we shall be completely at ease with you, with your undertakings and resolutions, and in harmony and devoted to ourselves and our equal Christians, and those that you are devoted to Lord. This is the character of devotion and it is your benevolence that imparts it in us Lord.

Lord, you have shown that you are our genuine harmony, and our guardian, enfolding us through our tribulation and persistently undertaking to ascend us into infinite rest. So when your forgiveness and benevolence have made us meek and mild we shall be totally secure. As there is no wrath in you Lord the soul that is genuinely in harmony with itself is immediately in unison with you. Lord, you desire us to discern that when we are overflowing with harmony and devotion, we are not hostile to you, and no manifestation of the discord that abides in us now- assuredly your benevolence transforms it all to our benefit. Lord Jesus, you take all the tribulation and anguish that have resulted from our defiance and ascend them to your heavenly abode, where you transform them into more delight and agreement than our emotions could discern or we could speak of.

Lord, when you ascend us into your heavenly abode we shall discover them prepared, renewed into genuine blessing and continuous exaltation. Thus Lord, you are our unshakeable foundation. You are our total rapture, and in your heavenly abode you will transform us as you are-steadfast! Amen.

CHAPTER 50

How the guilt of our iniquity constantly remains over us. In God's perception the higher entity that is going to be redeemed has never expired and never will expire.

Lord God, Heavenly Father, you have shown that in our temporal life your compassion and absolution guide our steps and they continually lead us to benevolence. As a result of the trials and tribulations into which we permit ourselves to decline, by temporal rules we are frequently considered to have expired; but in your beholding Lord the soul, which is going to be redeemed, has never expired and never will expire.

Benevolent Lord, you have shown that you are genuine devotion: in our temporal life we are gravely iniquitous and are immense in our shortcoming. But Lord, we never behold that you on any account condemn us in any form. How can this be?

Benevolent Lord, you have shown that you associate no greater condemnation to us than to the virtuous and righteous angels in your heavenly abode. Amen.

CHAPTER 51

How the Lord is the master and we are his attendants. Our Father does not propose to condemn us for more than he condemned his own adored and beloved Son.

Lord God, you have shown with a wondrous clarification of a master who has an attendant. The master is residing in splendour, meekly and serenely; the attendant is upright honourably in front of him, prepared to carry out his desires. The master beholds his attendant very devotedly and compassionately, and meekly dismisses him to carry out the master's affairs.

Out of his devotion for his master the attendant goes to complete his master's wishes. He falls, however, into a deep pit and is grievously harmed; he is helpless. He is without comfort as a result of not being able to behold his master, who is devoted to him and has all the solace that he longs for. But he makes the mistake of concentrating on his emotions and so he has anguish.

In his affliction he endures seven immense anguishes. The first is austere and immensely grievous from his stumble, the second is the measure of his entity; the third the following frailty; the fourth is that his discernment is mixed up and his intellect disturbed nearly forgetting his devotion; the fifth is that he is unable to get up; and the sixth is that he is abandoned. The seventh anguish is that this abode is unfathomable, disagreeable and abhorrent. The master beholds the attendant in two ways: first externally in tenderness and lowliness with immense mercy and understanding. Secondly the master has bliss as a result of the exalted transformation through his overflowing benevolence that he wants for his attendant.

It is as if this benevolent master was pronouncing that the attendant suffered out of his devotion for the master. The master discerns that he should compensate him for his suffering. Also he discerns that he should add a more immense reward than he has ever had.

Lord, you have shown that you wish us to discern and believe that you will show all entireties according to your ordination, benevolence, and for your undertaking.

Lord, through this wondrous clarification you have shown that the master is you, and Adam was the attendant. This was to show Lord that you discern all humanity as one and their decline as one. The attendant declined at his peak and was totally debilitated, and his intellect was confused so that he stopped beholding his master. But you wish us to discern Lord that the attendant's will was kept complete and secure. The attendant did not discern this, which resulted in great anguish and affliction. Not only was he unable to behold his master clearly, even though his master was devoted to him with tenderness and lowliness, he could not behold himself as his master beheld him. Lord, when these two are truly beheld we shall have repose and tranquillity- starting now and in total bliss when we are in your heavenly abode, through overflowing benevolence.

Lord, you have shown that it is only our anguish that condemns and chastises, while you impart solace and sympathy with us. In your devotion you yearn to ascend us to your bliss.

Lord, your mercy and understanding are for the decline of your divine creation; Adam; the bliss and rapture are for your divine Son who is identical to you. Therefore your forgiveness and understanding abide with humanity until at last we are ascended into your heavenly abode.

Lord, you have shown that you selected man's soul to be your own city and abode. But when Adam declined into remorse and anguish, he became unsuitable to receive your exaltation. You would not select anywhere else for yourself. You abided until through your benevolence and grievous anguish, your divine Son had restored the city to a place of immense blessing again.

Lord, through this wondrous clarification you have shown your faithfulness and your beloved sanctity. Enfolded within yourself are all the heavens, and all infinite bliss and rapture. Lord, you have shown that you have immense rapture as a result of the exalted transformation, which in your overflowing benevolence you had planned for your creation.

Lord, you have shown that the attendant represents the second person of the Trinity and also for Adam, that is humanity. The Son means Christ in his sanctity, proportionate with you Lord and the attendant means Christ's mankind, which is the genuine Adam. The nearness of the attendant represents the Son, Jesus Christ, and the Holy Spirit is the devotion that abides in them proportionately.

Lord, when Adam declined (which is all humanity), your Son fell into the virgin's womb to relinquish Adam from all condemnation in your heavenly abode and on earth. Lord Jesus, with miraculous dominion you have ascended Adam from the abyss. Our righteousness and benevolence are imparted from you Lord Jesus, our shortcomings and lack of vision from Adam.

Lord, you have shown that you do not resolve to condemn mankind anymore than you condemned your beloved Son. For all those souls that are going to be redeemed through Jesus' divine manifestation and Passion is enfolded in Christ's humanity; he is the head and we are elements of his body. Lord Jesus, in you we can behold the immense yearning and will of all humanity who are ready to be redeemed: for you Lord Saviour are all who are going to be redeemed and all who are to be redeemed are you. This is imparted by you Lord God, and, through our undertaking, reverence, meekness, persistence and other righteousness.

Lord, you have shown that after our Lord Jesus had fallen into the virgin's womb he could never ascend once more in all his dominion until his humanity had been destroyed and had expired. He then had to submit his soul into your dominion Lord; alongside with all humanity to whom he had been sent.

Lord, you have shown that our Lord Jesus Christ now sits on the illustrious throne which he created in your heavenly abode to his total contentment, with inestimable honour upon his head. Lord, you have shown that humanity is his crowning honour, and that this honour is your bliss, the Son's exaltation, the Holy Spirit's rapture, and the eternal joy of all the company of heaven.

Lord Jesus, you sit at our Lord God's right hand in continual solace and repose, in the position of the most elevated eminence and distinction in the rapture of our

Lord God, Heavenly Father. Lord Jesus, you are the true Son of God and true humanity, you can reside tranquilly and contentedly in your dominion which our Lord God undertook should be yours before time began; and Lord God you are in the Son and the Holy Spirit is in you and the Son. Amen.

CHAPTER 52

How we now have cause to grieve, for our iniquity led to Christ's affliction.

Lord God, Heavenly Father, you have shown that you have rapture because you are our father and our mother; and rapture because you are our genuine husband and our soul is your devoted wife. And Christ has bliss because he is our brother and Jesus has rapture, as he is our saviour. Lord, you desire us to discern that these are the five exalted raptures, that you wish us to have bliss in as we give you exaltation, gratitude, devotion and honour for infinity.

In our temporal life those who are going to be redeemed are a miraculous blend of benevolence and iniquity. Our ascended Lord Jesus Christ you abide in us, alongside the baseness and injury as a result of Adam's decline and expiring. Lord Jesus, as you impart your benevolence we are enfolded safely so that we are ascended and we are sure of our redemption; by Adam's decline we are fragmented within ourselves. We are fragmented in various aspects and thrust into such gloom through iniquity and diverse anguishes that we can barely find any solace. But our resolution is to remain with you Lord God, assuredly believing that you will impart forgiveness and benevolence- and this is undertaking in us. In your benevolence you give us discernment and we have inner beholding- occasionally to a greater extent, occasionally to a lesser extent, depending on the capability you impart us to accept it.

Lord, as a consequence we become so confused that our emotions are so perplexed and barely discern where we or our equal-Christians' position is- apart from answering yes to you when we do feel your presence. By answering 'yes'- this inner resolution that we are yours, in character and in essence with all our might. That is when we abhor our iniquitous resolutions and all that could make us iniquitous, in our entity and devotedly. But as this presence is withdrawn we descend into gloom again, and into all manner of remorse and anguish. Lord Jesus at this time we believe that as our guardian we shall never succumb to the gloom, but suffer under it and keep going, in affliction and remorse, beseeching you Lord God until you impart your presence once more.

Lord, throughout our temporal life we are in this confusion. But Lord, it is your desire that we discern that you are always beside us. You impart your presence in three ways: first in your heavenly abode- and you ascend us into your presence. Second, you impart your presence in our temporal life, guiding us. And third, you abide in our soul, leading us and protecting us.

So Lord, in the clarification you showed the harm and lack of vision as a result of Adam's decline and the enlightenment and benevolence of your Son. Through your Son you have imparted your mercy and tenderness for Adam's anguish, and the sovereign eminence and the dominion of the passion and expiring of your Son's humanity have bestowed infinite exaltation to mankind. Lord Jesus, you have immense rapture regarding man's decline because of the elevation that we shall be ascended to and the total rapture we shall encounter that transcends anything we would have encountered if we had not declined.

Lord, as a consequence of this we should be in sorrow, for our iniquity resulted in Christ's anguish, but we also have an infinite rapture for his unending devotion made him endure the anguish. So Lord, if by benevolence we behold your undertaking of devotion we abhor nothing but iniquity, for you have shown that devotion and abhorrence are absolutely incompatible. Lord, you desire us to discern that in our temporal life we shall understand the virtue and deliverance from iniquity that we shall encounter in your heavenly abode. But by benevolence we may triumph in averting ourselves from the iniquity that results in infinite anguish, as Holy Church discerns to us, and we may have the fortitude to avert slight iniquities.

Lord, if our lack of vision and gloom cause us to decline at any time we can soon ascend again under your tender presence of benevolence, and with our resolution change our direction, led by the discernment of Holy Church depending on the severity of the iniquity. We should acknowledge our shortcomings, saying that we would not survive for a moment without your benevolence Lord, and we should devotedly hold on to you, believing only in you.

Lord, you have shown that we should meekly blame ourselves; only you in your benevolence can absolve us. Lord, you showed this in the two ways that you beheld the decline of your devoted attendant. The first was the exterior, in meekness and humbleness, with immense mercy and tenderness, coming from infinite devotion. You desire us to blame ourselves- earnestly and genuinely acknowledging our decline and the injury it has caused, and discerning that alone we can never justify it; earnestly and genuinely acknowledging your infinite devotion for us and your abundant forgiveness. This self-blame that you expect from us Lord is that through your benevolence you meekly enfold both of these together. For Lord you undertake in our base character. Secondly Lord is the exalted restitution that you have imparted for man.

The second way that you beheld us Lord was our inmost entity. It was a more elevated division.

The entity and dominion that we possess in our base character is imparted by benevolence from the elevated, and from the elevated self's character devotion. There is no contrast between the entity and dominion that are in our elevated and base character: they all come from the same devotion. This devout devotion undertakes in us in two ways. In our base character there are anguishes and fervour, compassion and absolution, and other benevolence. In the elevated character these are absent, there is only the outstanding devotion and miraculous rapture in which all anguish is cured. Benevolent Lord, here you have shown that we are not only pardoned from condemnation (as you behold our elevated character) but also the exalted eminence which you will ascend us by the undertaking of your grace in our base nature when you shall transform all our dishonour into infinite exaltation. Amen.

CHAPTER 53

For in every higher entity that is going to be redeemed there is a godly desire that has never succumbed to iniquity, or ever will. Before our God created us he was devoted to us, as we are devoted to him.

Lord God, Heavenly Father, you desire us to discern that you have no less detrimental emotions about the decline of those of mankind who are going to be redeemed than you had over the decline of Adam. For Lord, you are so benevolent, compassionate and affectionate that you never condemn those who will honour and exalt you for infinity.

Lord, you have shown with total surety that dwelling in every soul that is going to be redeemed there is a godly desire that has never succumbed to iniquity, or ever will. That devoted will never desires iniquity, only what is benevolent in your beholding. Lord, you desire us to discern that we should acknowledge this as a certainty of Christian belief particularly with faith that our devoted will is securely enfolded by our Lord Jesus Christ. Lord God, through your benevolence and in your infinite enlightenment you have ordained that mankind's devoted character will eventually furnish your heavenly abode, this fundamental character enfolded and in unison with you can never be put asunder from you.

Lord, you have ordained that regardless of this divine and infinite affinity and unison the salvation of humanity is needed and compelling.

Lord, you have always been devoted to your creation mankind and you have always undertaken for him in virtue. Lord Jesus, in total accordance of the Trinity it was your will to be the foundation and crown of this devoted character of mankind. We have been derived from you, in you we are protected and we are on our temporal path to be with you. The divine Trinity ordained before time began that the second person would be our complete rapture, in infinite bliss. Lord, before you created us you were devoted to us, as we were devoted to you. Our devoted character is formed from the Holy Spirit in his fundamental and innate benevolence. This devotion is indomitable through your indomitable domain Lord Father, and enlightened through the enlightenment of our Lord Jesus. Humanity's soul, therefore, was both created by you Lord God, and enfolded by you.

Lord, this fundamental character is in unison with your fundamental character. Nothing can come between you and humanity's soul. You secure man's soul wholly in this infinite devotion- and you guide us and guard us so that we shall never be eradicated. Lord, you desire us to discern that just as the soul exists, it shall have devotion, giving gratitude and exaltation for infinity in your heavenly abode through your benevolence and compassion. We have always been cherished and shrouded in you and discerned and devoted by you.

Lord, you desire us to discern that you consider mankind to be the most supreme entity of your creation, and its entire manifestation, proclaiming entire unbroken benevolence, is the divine soul Christ. You also desire us to discern that Christ's precious human soul was closely, complexly, and indomitably united to you and that through mankind's soul is in a divine union for infinity.

Lord, all the souls that are going to be infinitely redeemed in your heavenly abode are united to you in this affinity, and made righteous in this righteousness. Amen.

CHAPTER 54

How total belief is a flawless discernment united with an assurance and positive conviction deriving from our essential entity, that we abide in our Lord and he abides in us, even though we do not behold him.

Lord God, Heavenly Father, you have shown that in your immense and infinite devotion for all humanity, you ordain no contrast between the divine soul of Lord Jesus Christ, and the most inconsiderable soul to be redeemed. Lord, you desire us to discern that where our Lord Jesus' divine soul is, there too, in their fundamental entity, are all the souls who are going to be redeemed by him.

Lord, we should have bliss that you abide in our soul! Moreover, we should have immense bliss that our soul abides in you. Lord, our soul is created as your abiding-abode, and the soul's abiding-abode is you Lord, who is not created. Lord, it is our immense comfort to have a central promise that you, our maker, abide in our soul. Lord, it is an even more immense comfort to discern that our created soul abides in the fundamental entity of you! Our entity is because we come from your entity.

Lord, you desire us to discern that the entity is all you. Lord God, Heavenly Father, you created us and enfolded us in yourself and the Trinity, and we in you and the Trinity: all-powerful, all-enlightenment, all benevolence, one God, one Lord.

Lord, you have shown that our faith is a righteousness

that is imparted from our inborn fundamental entity into our carnal character through the Holy Spirit, and it is through belief that all other righteousness is imparted, for no one can encounter any righteousness without belief. Total belief is a flawless discernment united with a genuine assurance and positive conviction deriving from our essential entity, that we abide in you Lord and you abide in us, even though we do not behold you. Lord, through this righteousness and all other righteousness that are imparted with it, you undertake immense acts in us. Lord Jesus, you undertake through us by your compassion, and in benevolence we give ourselves to you through the bequests and dominion of the Holy Spirit. Lord Jesus, this undertaking in us, creates us as your children, and empowers us to live Christian lives. Amen.

CHAPTER 55

How Christ is our path, guiding us securely. Humanity had to be reverted back from expiring in two parts.

Lord God, Heavenly Father, you have shown that Christ is our path, guiding us securely by his commandments, and in his entity mightily ascending us up to your heavenly abode. Lord Jesus, you devotedly bestow all those whom you will redeem to your heavenly Father. Lord God, you thankfully receive this offering and then graciously return it to our Lord Jesus Christ. This offering and acknowledgement impart bliss to the Trinity. Lord, it gives you most rapture to behold us having rapture in the divine Trinity's bliss over our redemption. Lord, you desire us to discern and embrace by belief, that our genuine existence is in your heavenly abode rather than in our temporal life.

Lord, you have shown that our belief results from the essential devotion of our soul, from the enlightenment of our intellect and from the immovable aspiration that you imparted to us in our creation. Lord, when you instil our soul into our entity, causing our faculties to awaken, then forgiveness and benevolence instantly start to undertake, considering us and giving us sanctuary with tenderness and devotion. At this juncture the Holy Spirit receives our belief and develops the anticipation that when we have flourished and transformed into wisdom in the Holy Spirit, we shall revert to our fundamental entity in your heavenly abode, to the mighty benevolence of our Lord Jesus Christ. Through this Lord you have shown that our incarnate character has its foundation in your character, forgiveness, and benevolence- a foundation that empowers us to accept offerings that guide us to infinite entity.

Lord, you have shown with total assurance that our entity is in you. You are also in our incarnate character, too. Lord, from the commencement of time you have decreed that from the instant that we become incarnate entity, at that juncture we would become the city of God. Lord, you abide there for infinity with immense rapture. Lord, all your offerings to us are imparted to our Lord Jesus on our behalf. Lord Jesus, as you abide in us you possess these offerings within yourself, until we are transformed in our character into wisdom. The Holy Spirit is then able to undertake in forgiveness in our innermost character, in his benevolence instilling into us offerings that guide us to infinite entity.

Lord, you desire us to discern that you have formed our souls as a trinity similar to the rapturous uncreated Trinity. Lord, you have discerned this, been devoted to and in unison with this from the commencement of time.

As a result of this exalted unison between the soul and our entity, ordained by you Lord, humanity had to be reverted back from an expiring in two parts. This return could not occur until you Lord Jesus Christ, who were in unison with our elevated character when it was first formed, had also acquired our base nature. These two characters established one soul in you Lord Jesus. The elevated character was in unison and tranquillity with you Lord God, overflowing with bliss and rapture; the base character, the incarnate character, had anguish for the redemption of humanity.

Lord, you have shown that this essential, elevated character, that this entity is the sovereign entity, the beloved soul of Christ, who has ceaseless rapture in the nature and condition of being God. Amen.

CHAPTER 56

How God is closer to us than our own higher entity. If we desire to discern our higher entity we must search for it, for it is in God in whom it is embraced.

Lord God, Heavenly Father, you have shown with total assurance that we could discern you with less difficulty than we could our own soul. For our own soul has its immense foundation in you and is infinitely cherished by you that we cannot discern it until we first discern you, who formed it, to whom it is in unison with. Lord, you desire that we have an enlightened true will to discern our own soul. We must look for it where it is: in you. Through the guidance and benevolence of the Holy Spirit we shall discern them together. It is devoted and genuine, and of no consequence whether we feel we wish to discern you Lord, or our soul.

Lord, you are closer to us than our own soul, for you are the foundation of our soul on whom our soul trusts in, and you are the focus that stops our fundamental entity and our carnal character from being apart. Our soul abides in you in genuine repose, and is upright in your genuine might; it is certainly founded in you in infinite devotion. So if we desire to discern our soul, to converse with it, to debate with it, we must search for it in you in whom it is embraced.

Lord, our fundamental entity, and our carnal character

can justly be named our soul, as a result of their unison with you.

Lord Jesus, your exalted city where you have your dominion is our carnal character and you are enfolded in it, and our essential entity is enfolded in you. It abides in your divine soul as you are settled in tranquillity in the nature and condition of being God.

Lord God, you have shown with immense assurance that we should have yearning and repentance until we are guided so profoundly into you that we genuinely and absolutely discern our own soul. Our benevolent Lord Jesus, you have genuinely shown that it is you who guide us into this immeasurable wisdom with the same devotion that you created us and ransomed us in forgiveness and benevolence through the dominion of your divine Passion.

But regardless of this we can never truly discern you Lord until we have discerned our own soul. For until the soul is completely wise we cannot be truly divine. This will only come to pass, when through the dominion of your holy Passion Lord Jesus, our carnal character is ascended to the distinction of our fundamental being, and when Lord Jesus in your forgiveness and benevolence have empowered it to gain from all the teachings of its anguishes.

Lord God, benevolence and forgiveness are derived from your fundamental character and are infused into us, bringing all undertakings to our pure bliss. This is the foundation from which we develop and find accomplishment. Lord, it is your desire that we discern that there are three attributes in benevolence, and when one is undertaking in our temporal life, all are undertaking. We should wish to discern these attributes in more and more immense wisdom until we are made pure.

To completely discern these attributes is akin to the infinite rapture, and the endless bliss in your heavenly abode. Lord, in our temporal lives you desire us to begin to discern your heavenly abode as we encounter your devotion.

Lord, you have shown that we cannot achieve this by our own intellect, but only if there is purpose and devotion as well. Also we cannot be redeemed if we discern you only as the foundation of our character, but only if we are imparted with forgiveness and benevolence from that foundation. For it is from these three undertakings in unison that we are imparted with all our benevolence. First we are imparted with the essential benevolent offerings, for when you formed us Lord you bestowed as much benevolence as we could accept, and then a more immense benevolence, in our soul alone. Lord, it was in your divine determination and infinite enlightenment that you desired that we should have two characters. Amen.

CHAPTER 57

How in Christ our fundamental character and lower character are bound together.

Lord God, Heavenly Father, in our fundamental character, you created us with such eminence and magnificence that those that are going to be redeemed always carry out your desires and impart exaltation to you. Lord, you have enabled us to do this through the immense treasure and glorious righteousness that you imparted to the soul when you joined it to our temporal entity. In our fundamental character, we are pure, in our lower character we have our shortcomings. Lord, you shall restore these shortcomings through your benevolent character.

Lord, you have shown that our complete character is in you and various parts of it stem from you to achieve your desires. Lord Jesus, you were united to our lower character when you took our mortality. In you Lord Jesus, both characters are bound together. Lord Jesus, you are within the Trinity, so our fundamental character is founded in you, while you as the second person, are bound in our lower character which was formed for you. Out of your benevolence you ordained to become humanity.

Lord, our belief is the start of other gifts. Through your essential character you impart forgiveness and benevolence and from this our belief is imparted from our fundamental entity to our lower character.

Lord, you have shown that you desire us to discern your commandments in two ways: first there are your decrees which we should be devoted to and adhered to and second your constraints. We should know what you inhibit and we should abhor and repel them.

Lord; together with our belief are the seven sacraments, and every type of righteousness. Lord, the righteousness that has been imparted to us from our fundamental entity, were a gift in your benevolence, and are also imparted and sustained in us by the Holy Spirit undertaking in forgiveness and benevolence. This righteousness and bequests are held as treasures for us in you Lord Jesus. For when you took our temporal character, you held our entire entity within yourself, thereby enfolding our higher entity, and so becoming perfect man. Our Lady is our mother, and in you Lord Jesus we are all enfolded in her and born from her. Lord Jesus, as our redeemer we are enfolded in you and always shall be and so you are our mother.

Lord God, you have shown that you abide in our soul. It is your immense rapture to have your dominion here with our discernment, and to infinitely abide in tranquillity, undertaking to ascend us all to yourself. Lord, you have shown that you desire for us to aid you in this undertaking, by imparting our contemplation, discerning your teachings, abiding by your commandments, wishing to undertake everything you undertake and believing you genuinely.

Lord, you have clearly shown that our fundamental character is in you! Amen.

CHAPTER 58

How our complete entity is firstly our temporal character, the second forgiveness, and the third benevolence. The immense dominion of the Trinity is our Father, the infinite enlightenment of the Trinity is our Mother, and the eminent devotion of the Trinity is our Lord.

Lord God, Heavenly Father, you have shown that the holy Trinity, who is infinite entity ordained before time to create humanity. Our adorable temporal character was made for your own Son, the second person, and when you ordained, with the accord of the whole Trinity, you made us all at once. Lord, when you made us you enfolded us to yourself making us one with you. Through this unison you keep us as innocent and as eminent as when we were first created. Lord, it is by the dominion of that cherished unison that we can be devoted to you and search for you, give you exaltation, gratitude and infinitely have rapture in you. Lord, it is your beloved desire to undertake in this manner for every soul that is going to be redeemed.

Lord God, you have shown that when you created us, you were the Father of our temporal character, God all-enlightenment our Mother, and in union were the devotion and benevolence of the Holy Spirit and this is all one God, one Lord. Lord, it is your desire that this unison be as a husband and wife, and to us your wife, you never have any anguish. This devotion between us shall never be separated.

Lord, you have shown that through the attributes of the holy Trinity, you protect us in three ways. Lord God, you have protected our fundamental entity in bliss since you made us. Our temporal character is protected, renewed and redeemed by you Lord Jesus. The Holy Spirit gives us honour and compensation for our temporal trials and tribulation, which is greater than we could ever wish for.

Our complete entity is firstly our temporal character, the second, forgiveness, and the third, benevolence.

Lord God, your immense dominion is in the Trinity as our Father, the infinite enlightenment of the Trinity is our Mother, and the eminent devotion of the Trinity is our Lord. This was imparted to us when our fundamental entity was formed.

Lord Jesus, as the beloved second person of the holy Trinity, you are Mother to our fundamental entity, in which we have our foundation. You have also become Mother in relation to our temporal character, that you took out of your forgiveness, for Lord God, you created us in two divisions, fundamental entity, and temporal character. Our fundamental entity is our elevated character. So Lord Jesus, you are our Mother to our two characters, which are not separated. Lord Jesus through you we flourish and mature; in your forgiveness you chasten and renew us; and by the dominion of your Passion, temporal extinction and rebirth you enfold us to our fundamental entity. Lord Jesus, as our Mother, this is how you undertake in forgiveness for all those compliant and dutiful children.

Lord, you have shown that benevolence undertakes with forgiveness. The undertaking of the Holy Spirit is through enriching and imparting to us. Lord, the honour that you give to your servant who has endured anguish, is the eminent bestowing of inner integrity. You impart this devotedly and voluntarily in your benevolence, completing and surpassing all that we are worthy of.

Lord, you have shown that our complete fundamental entity is in each person of the Trinity, who is one God, but our temporal character is only in you Lord Jesus, as the second person of the Trinity. Lord God, you and the Holy Spirit are in our Lord Jesus and through you Lord Jesus we have mightily been rescued from hell and out of the baseness of the earth and exaltedly ascended into your heavenly abode. In your heavenly abode we have advanced in abundance and eminence, by the dominion of you Lord

Jesus Christ, and by the benevolence and undertaking of the Holy Spirit. Amen.

CHAPTER 59

How our Lord Jesus, who reciprocates benevolence for iniquity, is our genuine Mother. We have our entity from him, the foundation and beginning of all motherhood, and alongside that we have all the affectionate guardianship for infinity.

Lord God, you have shown that this immense rapture is imparted through forgiveness and benevolence and we could never have discerned or have been blessed by it if that devotion in you had not been challenged; it is through this challenge that we have our rapture. Iniquity was permitted to go against devotion; and the devotion of benevolence and forgiveness went against that iniquity, turning it into devotion and exaltation for those who are going to be redeemed. Lord God, it is in your entity to reciprocate benevolence for iniquity, so Lord Jesus as you reciprocate benevolence for iniquity, you are our genuine Mother. We have our entity from you, the foundation and beginning of all motherhood, and alongside that we have all the affectionate devotional guardianship for infinity.

Lord God, you have shown that you are genuinely our Mother as you are our Father. You showed in your affection that you are the entity, the dominion, and benevolence of fatherhood; the enlightenment of motherhood; the illumination and benevolence of divine devotion, the Trinity; the unison; the ruler of benevolence of every entity; you empower us to have devotion, to yearn; you are the infinite contentment of all genuine longings.

Lord, you have ordained that the soul is most supreme, most elevated and immense, when it is meek, mild and tender. As an offering from our fundamental entity in you, you impart all the righteousness to our lower entity; assisted and guided by forgiveness and benevolence that empowers us to accomplish your ordinations. You ordained the second person of the Trinity should become our Mother, Lord Jesus you achieved it, the Holy Spirit rooted it in us.

Lord, you have shown that our entity comes from character, forgiveness and benevolence. From these you imparted humbleness and tenderness, forbearance and compassion. You also imparted through these our abhorrence of iniquity and wretchedness, for you ordained that it is in the character of righteousness to abhor these.

Lord Jesus, you are our true Mother in character because of our first formation, and you are our genuine Mother in benevolence because you took our lower character. In you Lord Jesus, abides all the devoted undertaking and affectionate instinctive guardianship that abides in devoted motherhood, and through you our desires for God are always complete and protected, both spontaneously and by benevolence, because of your fundamental devotion.

Lord God, you have shown that you desire us to discern the motherhood of God in three ways. The first is your formation of our lower character; the second your embracing of our character- from which flows the motherhood of benevolence; and the third is the applied undertaking of motherhood, as a consequence and by that same benevolence, it reaches out in infinite stature, magnitude, measure and intensity. And all is one in devotion. Amen.

CHAPTER 60

Lord Jesus is our essential benevolent Mother.

Lord God, Heavenly Father, you have shown that through this reaching out, we are returned by the motherhood of forgiveness and benevolence into our essential place.

Lord Jesus Christ, as you desired to become our Mother in our lower character and our Mother in benevolence, you began in total humbleness and tenderness, in the virgin's womb. Here you took on our weak entity, and were totally ready to take on motherhood with all the undertaking and labour.

Lord Jesus, nobody could have carried out this undertaking so completely, except you. You are all devotion and you carry us for rapture and infinite entity. We impart our exaltation to you! You enfold us in devotion, and your labour endured the most excruciating anguishes and the cruellest birth pains imaginable, until the lower entity that you had taken on expired. Even though you had given birth to us for our infinite bliss, you have shown that if you could have endured any more anguish for us you would have.

Lord Jesus, your undertaking continues with the supreme, gentle affection as our divine Mother you carry on sustaining us with your body and blood in the divine communion, with infinite forgiveness and benevolence. Through you we have the well being of the divine communion, all the righteousness and benevolence of your word, all your devotion set-aside for us in Holy Church.

Lord Jesus, you guide us tenderly into your divine breast, through the tender open wound in your side, and there you momentarily show the Godhead and the rapture of your heavenly abode, with the inmost assurance of infinite rapture.

Lord Jesus, this affectionate, devoted word *Mother* is so akin to the centre of our entity that it should only be used in relation to you and to your mother, who is the mother to us all. The devotion in entity, enlightenment, discernment and benevolence are akin with motherhood. Our natural birth is minute, inconsequential, and easy in comparison with our spiritual birth, and yet Lord God you bring about our natural birth. An essential, devoted mother who discerns and recognises the longings of her child will care for him with total gentleness. As her child grows she changes her ways but not her devotion, and as he grows even more she allows him to be chastised in order to correct him and show him how to accept righteousness and benevolence. Lord, you have shown that this is your undertaking along with all that is gracious and benevolent- in those who abide in this manner.

Lord God, you have shown that by your benevolence, you are the essential Mother of our lower character, out of devotion for our higher character. Lord, you desire us to discern this for you wish us to cleave all our devotion on to you. Through this you have shown that every undertaking that you have imparted to us to exalt fatherhood and motherhood, is achieved as we are genuinely devoted to you who are our Father and our Mother, and Lord Jesus, you infuse this sacred devotion in us. Lord God, you are the one we are devoted to. Amen.

CHAPTER 61

How in our heavenly abode we shall behold the extent of our iniquity in our temporal life, but also behold how our Creator's devotion for us never altered. This devotion will never be altered, and is as a consequence powerful and awesome.

Lord Jesus Christ, you have shown that with regard to our spiritual birth, you take care of us with supreme gentleness as you behold our soul as much more valuable. You inspire our discernment, guide our direction, console our moral sense, comfort our soul, and give enlightenment to our heart. You empower us to be devoted to everything that you are devoted to, and to be completely contented with you and all your undertakings. When we are fortified by your benevolence we then follow you as your attendant and are devoted to you for infinity.

Lord, you allow our shortcomings so that we can behold how weak and iniquitous we are in ourselves. In your heavenly abode we shall behold the extent of our iniquity in our temporal life, but also behold how our Creator's devotion for us never altered. This devotion will never be altered, and is as a consequence powerful and awesome. When we behold our shortcomings we are imparted with humbleness and tenderness, this ascends us in your heavenly abode to an extent that we might never have attained.

Lord Jesus Christ, as the Mother of our heavenly abode, you will never let your children perish, for you are all powerful, all enlightenment, and all devotion. No one compares with you. We give you exaltation!

Lord Jesus, when we behold our shortcomings and iniquity, we are scared and so terribly embarrassed that we hardly know where to hide. But Lord Jesus as our gentle Mother you do not want us to go; you abhor nothing greater. You have shown that you desire us to turn to you as a small child would turn to its mother for comfort whenever it needed it. Your desire is for us to declare, 'My gentle affectionate Mother, please give me ransom. I'm iniquitous- and I don't compare to you in any way. I am helpless to alter this- I yearn for your comfort and benevolence.'

Lord Jesus, in your enlightenment you may behold that it is more appropriate for us to be downcast and emotional, and in your benevolence for us you will permit this, and with mercy and kindness, until the appropriate moment. You desire us to be like a devoted child who always has faith in his mother's devotion in happy times and in sad times.

Lord Jesus, you have shown that it is your desire that we have powerful belief in the Holy Church, and with all the assembly of the saints behold our devoted Mother by the church, and discern the solace that is imparted from genuine enlightenment. Our body may frequently feel overpowered, but the complete entity of the church is indestructible. And so it is a secure and gracious undertaking, and a way of benevolence, to desire to be meekly in unison with our Mother Holy Church who is you Lord Jesus. The cherished blood and water that you pour over us in your forgiveness is ample to make us whole and righteous. Lord Jesus, your divine wounds are open to us, and you are rapturous to cure us; your affectionate, benevolent imparting hands as our Mother are always prepared to immensely undertake for us.

Lord Jesus, you have shown that it is your undertaking to redeem us; it is your exaltation to undertake this; and it is your desire that we should discern it so that we may be devoted to you tenderly and have meek and total belief in you. Amen.

CHAPTER 62

How God is the Father and Mother of all genuine character, and every character that he has imparted from himself to execute his ordinations will, when humanity is redeemed, be renewed and returned to him through his undertaking of benevolence.

Lord God, Heavenly Father, you have shown all the shortcomings that could possibly occur in this temporal entity. Simultaneously you have shown your divine dominion, enlightenment and devotion. You have shown that you protect us for your exaltation, compassionately and affectionately in all the phases of our temporal entity, benevolent and iniquitous. Through all our tribulations you ascend our higher entity high into your heavenly abode changing all to your exaltation and our bliss for infinity. In your benevolence all our temporal entity is of consequence.

Lord, this stems from the essence of your graciousness through your undertaking of benevolence. Lord, the essence of your character is fundamentally all benevolence. You are the foundation of all entity, the heart of what is genuine character. You are the Father and Mother of all genuine character, and every character that you have imparted from yourself to execute your ordination will, when humanity is redeemed, be renewed and returned to you through your undertaking of benevolence.

Lord, you have imparted various characters in all your created living entities, but in humanity all the divisions are in unison. Humanity's character is complete, with all its dominion. You have created it totally exquisite, benevolent, sovereign and gracious. It is all that is elevated, cherished and exalted.

Lord, through all this we can behold that we owe you for our character and for your benevolence, and we do not have to look far to discern all the characters, but only need to behold Holy Church, our Mother's breast, which is our fundamental entity, and your abode. There we shall behold everything we are looking for- beholding it now in belief and by our intellect but in eternity distinctly and rapturously in you Lord.

Lord, you have shown that you have ordained this not for one man, but as a universal rule and this relates to you our cherished Christ. This gracious temporal character was created for you Lord Jesus so that humanity could be formed in exaltation and exquisiteness and redeemed for rapture and blessedness. Lord God, you beheld this with enlightenment and discernment from the very outset. Amen.

CHAPTER 63

How iniquity is utterly against our gracious fundamental character. It is perverse, as it is impure. Our Lord shall restore our fundamental entity to affection and meekness.

Lord God, Heavenly Father, through all this we should behold that it is right for us to abhor iniquity- because of your benevolence and because it is in our fundamental character to abhor it. Benevolence returns our gracious temporal character to the abode it came from- to you Lord- with immense eminence and exaltation because benevolence undertakes with such dominion for devotion. Lord, all your divine children shall behold it- they have infinite rapture that their fundamental character have been found totally pure. So fundamental character and benevolence are in unison, for benevolence is you Lord and so is uncreated fundamental character. Lord, you are all one in devotion, you undertake in two ways- but benevolence and fundamental character do not undertake without the other- they cannot be apart.

Lord, through your benevolence and undertaking, if we live in unison with our fundamental character and benevolence, we should genuinely behold that iniquity is far worse and gives greater anguish than hell itself, for iniquity is utterly against our gracious fundamental character. It is as perverse as it is impure. It is an abhorrent beholding for the gracious fundamental entity who desires- as fundamental character and benevolence discern- to be all gracious and luminous before you Lord.

Lord, you have shown, however, that iniquity should not cause us anxiety- unless it is the sort of anxiety that drives us on. Lord Jesus, we should meekly call out to you our devoted Mother and you shall let your cherished blood flow over us. You shall restore our fundamental entity to affection and meekness; you shall cure us through your ordination that undertakes to impart immense exaltation to you and to us infinite rapture. Lord Jesus, you shall never abandon nor disdain this affectionate and gracious undertaking until all your devoted flock are born and returned to you. Lord Jesus, you showed this as your divine yearning, which is the devoted- yearning that will continue until the Day of Judgement.

Lord Jesus, through this you have shown that our entity is founded in you, our genuine Mother, through your infinite enlightenment and discernment beforehand, with the sovereign domain of our Father and the crowning benevolence of the Holy Spirit. Lord, by adopting our character you imparted to us our entity; through your Passion you have taken us to infinite entity. You constantly impart this to us and undertake for us- you do all this in your gracious mother's character and for the fundamental yearning of your flock.

Lord Jesus, our fundamental entity beholds you as our affectionate and gracious heavenly Mother; and you our heavenly Mother behold your flock as cherished, gracious and benevolent. Your flock is meek and mild with all the gracious fundamental characteristics of a child. It is not fundamentally right for the child to tire of his mother's devotion, or depend on himself; it is fundamentally right for him to be devoted to his mother and all your flock. Lord; through these gracious characteristics and others akin to them, we attend you as our heavenly Mother and impart to you rapture.

Lord God, you have shown that in our temporal entity we are so frail and inadequate, both in our intellect and in our body. We cannot ascend above the condition of a child, until you Lord Jesus, our devoted Mother, ascend us up into our Father's rapture. Then Lord God, you shall show the genuine discernment of how everything shall be agreeable. Your children shall behold for themselves, that everything shall be agreeable! Then Lord Jesus, the total bliss of you our Mother, shall start afresh in the rapture of our Father: a start that will always be fresh.

Lord God, you have shown that all your divine children have been given entity from your fundamental character and shall be returned to your heavenly abode through your benevolence. Amen.

THE FIFTEENTH REVELATION

CHAPTER 64

The Fifteenth Revelation shows that when our lower entity expires those who are going to be redeemed will be ascended out of all their anguish and all their infirmities. They will rise above to their heavenly abode, where they will be with our Lord Jesus and have total rapture and exaltation for infinity.

Lord God, Heavenly Father, you have shown that those who are going to be redeemed will be ascended out of their anguish, all their infirmities, all their anxieties, and all their sorrow. They will ascend above with you as their gift and shall overflow with devotion and rapture for infinity. They shall never again have any anguish of their will. You do not desire that we should be anxious over our temporal tribulation, as it is your ordination for your exaltation.

Lord, you have shown that you shall impart your gift of ascending your servants to your heavenly abode who persistently attend upon your ordination for the length of time that you require, and do not lose forbearance but make it endure over their temporal life. It is your desire that while our higher entity is in our temporal entity it senses that it could be ascended at any moment. All their burdensome temporal entity is transformed in that single moment from anguish to genuine and infinite rapture and the anguish that we have endured shall be of no consequence.

Lord, you have shown that out of the temporal entity on

the point of its expiry there will ascend a glorious creature, a small child, in all perfection, and purer than a lily, it shall float up into your heavenly abode.

Lord, you have shown that the expiry of the temporal entity and the decomposition of the body represent the immense iniquity of our temporal existence, and the small child represents the total innocence of our higher entity. The glory of the child imparts nothing on the temporal entity, and the child is not harmed in any way by the defilement of the temporal entity.

It is a rapturous promise and a complete assurance for a devoted higher entity to discern that we shall be ascended from anguish. Lord, through this promise you have shown that you have gracious tenderness for us in our enduring anguish, and your affectionate promise of total release. Lord, you desire that we contemplate this breathtaking rapture and be comforted.

Lord, it is your desire that we should contemplate this rapturous promises as frequently as we are able and to continue with it as long as we are able to. Lord, the higher entity that you guide to this contemplation has immense bliss, and for the duration of the contemplation it brings immense exaltation to you. When through our frailty we descend back into our accustomed apathy and divine lack of vision, lower entity and devout anguish, you desire us to recall your promise that you do not abandon us. You keep your undertaking that our anguish will end and we shall be ascended into rapture and exaltation for infinity.

Lord, you have shown that it is your desire that we should receive your promises and comforts with all the benevolence and fortitude that we possess, and simultaneously endure this passing of our temporal life with all its tribulations as readily as we are able. You desire us to disregard the tribulations as of no consequence. For the greater that our disregard for them out of our devotion for you Lord, and the less importance we bestow on them, the less anguish we shall endure, and the more immense our gratitude and gift because of them. Amen.

THE FIFTEENTH REVELATION

CHAPTER 65

How the benevolence of God imparts such unison in us that when we behold it no one can be departed from anyone else.

Lord God, Heavenly Father, you have shown that if we out of devotion purposely follow you in our temporal life, we can be confident that we have your infinite devotion: the infinite devotion imparts this benevolence in us. It is your desire that we be as confident of our aspiration of heavenly rapture in our temporal entity as we will be in your heavenly abode. The more immense rapture and bliss that this confidence gives us- combined with meekness and honour- the more rapture you have Lord. Our honour for you should be a devout esteemed awe in unison with graciousness, which is imparted when we behold you Lord as supremely exalted and ourselves as supremely minute.

This righteousness is the infinite imparting to those you are devoted to Lord, and through your benevolence it may in part be beheld and perceived in our temporal entity when we become conscious of your nearness. Lord, we immensely desire to perceive your nearness in all entity as this imparts in us a glorious feeling of protection, with genuine belief and complete assurance through your immense devotion, and with an affectionate and agreeable awe.

Lord, it is your desire that it is our obligation to behold ourselves to you in devotion as if all your ordinations and undertakings had only been imparted for each person alone. You impart such unison in us that when we behold it no one can be parted from any one else.

Lord, you have shown this that we might be devoted to you and give us discernment to be in awe of no entity but you. You desire us to perceive that you hold all the dominion of our enemy, and you are our comforter. We, who have this confidence, hold no other entity in awe, save you Lord to whom we are devoted. We should demote every other apprehension to a position among our feelings, bodily ailments or the illusions of the mind. As a consequence, though we may have immense anguish, tribulation and anxiety that it seems our intellect can focus on nothing but our poor condition, as early as we are able we cast it off and regard it as of no importance. How can we do this? We can do this Lord because if we discern you and are devoted to you, and devoutly are in awe of you, we shall have serenity and repose and everything that you undertake shall impart immense rapture to us. Amen.

THE SIXTEENTH REVELATION

The Sixteenth Revelation shows that our Lord Jesus Christ abides in the higher entity of those companions who have benevolence for him.

CHAPTER 66

I have not translated a prayer from chapter 66, as in it Julian describes a personal encounter with the Devil in her sleep.

THE SIXTEENTH REVELATION

CHAPTER 67

How our Lord Jesus will never depart his city within our higher entity. For here our Lord is totally at ease, we are his infinite abiding place. Our higher entity can never find repose in inferior entity- it can never have peace just beholding itself.

Lord God, Heavenly Father, you have shown our higher entity in the middle of our heart as immense as an unending world and appears as a rapturous domain. Its situation is that of an exalted city. Lord Jesus, you have the prominent position in the middle of our higher entity, as God and man, you are adorned as a glorious and awesome sovereign. You are immensely exalted on your throne within our higher entity with absolute tranquillity and repose. The Godhead has dominion and upholds the heavenly abode and earth and all entity- dominion strength, enlightenment and benevolence. Lord Jesus, you have shown that you will never depart your city within our higher entity. For here Lord you are totally at ease, we are your infinite abiding-place.

Lord Jesus, you have shown the contentment that was imparted to you to create our higher entity. Our Heavenly Father and you Lord Jesus exquisitely created our higher entity, which was the desire also of the Holy Spirit. As a consequence the Holy Trinity has constantly since the beginning, had rapture over the creation of our higher entity. He beheld that it would give him bliss for infinity.

Lord God, your creation of all entity shows your sovereignty. Lord, you have helped us discern this by imparting an example of a man who was permitted to behold all the exalted wealth and dominions ruled over by a lord. When he had beheld all the magnificence under his Lord then, overflowing with awe, he felt he should behold what was above, to the abode of the Lord himself, discerning that this would be the most supreme dominion of all.

Lord, through this you have shown that our higher entity can never find its repose in inferior entity. If it ascends above all formed entity into the self, it cannot have peace, just beholding itself. Rather its complete contemplation is centred rapturously on you Lord, our Creator, abiding within our higher entity. Our higher entity is the genuine abiding place of you Lord. You have shown that the most immense brilliance that illuminates our higher entity in the domain, is the exalted devotion of you our Lord God.

Lord, what could impart to us more immense rapture than for us to behold that you have immense rapture in us, the apex of all your formed entity? Lord, you have shown that the divine Trinity has, as far, as was able, created our higher entity as glorious and elevated. Lord, you desire our hearts to ascend above the abyssal parts of the earth; all hollow anguishes and have exaltation in you. Amen.

THE SIXTEENTH REVELATION

CHAPTER 68

How we may have an arduous passing; we may have affliction; and we may have trials, but we shall not be conquered in our temporal entity.

Lord Jesus Christ, if we in our higher entity contemplate you on your throne in the centre of our higher entity it will be a glorious enlightenment with tranquillity, and it will be wholesome to us. As we who contemplate this truth, are alike you who contemplate us, and by your benevolence we are silently and placidly in unison with you.

Lord, it will be a singular rapture for us to behold you sitting in our higher entity, for to sit down with tranquillity shows assurance and therefore stability. Lord Jesus, you have shown that you desire us not to consider this as a misapprehension, but you want us to be at ease with confidence. You desire us to acknowledge it, cleave to it, be comforted by it and believe it: you have shown Lord that we will not be conquered. Through your Passion you have shown that it is the devil that is overcome.

All this discernment with its genuine comfort relates to all our companions in you Lord Jesus, as is your ordination Lord God.

Lord, you have showed very emphatically and earnestly that we will not be conquered, this is to impart to us assurance and fortitude for every tribulation that we may encounter in our temporal entity. You know Lord that we may have an arduous passing; we may have affliction; and we may have trials, but we shall not be conquered in our temporal entity. Lord God, it is your desire that we give contemplation to this assurance so that we can constantly be resolute and fearless, through the agreeable and disagreeable periods of our temporal entity. You are devoted to us and have rapture in us, so you desire us to be devoted to you and have bliss in you and believe in you absolutely. So all will be agreeable. Amen.

THE SIXTEENTH REVELATION

CHAPTER 69

I have not written a prayer about this chapter because it relates to Julian's personal experience of the Devil.

THE SIXTEENTH REVELATION

CHAPTER 70

How God does not impart a greater benevolence that ascends more than belief, and there is no guidance in anything that is beneath it. Our Lord desires that we should remain within our belief.

Lord Jesus Christ, you have shown that it is your desire for us to discern that we should cleave to our faith in our hearts. It is your desire that our faith should remain with us to the end of our temporal life and then later be with us in total rapture. You desire us to always believe totally in your divine promise and to discern your benevolence.

Lord, our belief is antagonistic in various ways inwardly and outwardly by our short-sightedness and by our devotional opponent. Lord, you empower us by imparting devotional enlightenment and genuine discernment. You guide us both inwardly and outwardly- so that we may discern you. In whatever way your discernment comes, it is your desire that we should perceive you with enlightenment, accept you affectionately, and remain with you devotedly. Lord God, you have shown that you do not impart a greater benevolence that ascends more than belief, and there is no guidance in anything that is beneath it. We should remain within our belief and we have to cleave to it with the guidance of your benevolence and your undertaking in us. You permit our belief to be challenged by our devotional opponent to make it powerful, for if our belief had no opponent it would not merit any gift. Amen.

THE SIXTEENTH REVELATION

CHAPTER 71

How our Lord Jesus has three ways of beholding us.

Lord Jesus Christ, you have shown that your divine and glorious countenance to our higher entity has delight, bliss and affection. You constantly behold us as we exist with a yearning devotion to you. You desire our higher entity to veer to you readily to impart to you your honour. We pray that benevolence will remain to make our external behaviour comply more immensely with our essential entity and make us all in unison with you and with our companions in you, in the genuine and infinite rapture which is you Lord Jesus.

Lord Jesus, you have shown that you have three ways of beholding us. The first is the countenance on your face at your Passion when you were expiring in your human entity. Although this is immensely downcast and agitated, it is still animated because you are God. The second is affectionate forbearance and mercy, imparted with an affirmation of total guardianship to all that are devoted to you and cleave to you for forgiveness. The third is total and infinite rapture. You have shown that the third is the one that is imparted more often and lasts for the greatest length of time.

Lord Jesus, when we are in affliction and sorrow you impart to us the countenance of your Passion and cross, empowering us with your divine dominion to endure our tribulation. When we are in iniquity you impart to us the countenance of forbearance and mercy, as you mightily enfold and shield us from our opponent. These are the two accustomed ways of countenance that we behold in our temporal entity. But sometimes there is a third, the countenance of total rapture, which we behold briefly now, but will discern in your heavenly abode. Lord Jesus, this is imparted through your intimation of benevolence in the affectionate illumination of our higher entity and by it we are enfolded in certain assurance, longing and devotion, with penitence and dedication, with deliberation, and numerous encounters of genuine restoration and affectionate inspiration. Amen.

THE SIXTEENTH REVELATION

CHAPTER 72

How if we encounter with any form of iniquity we shall never behold God's countenance.

Lord God, Heavenly Father, you have shown that the two most immense conflicts are the greatest rapture and the gravest anguish. The greatest rapture is to be blessed with you Lord in the illumination of infinite entity, beholding you genuinely, being blessed by you entirely and encountering your affection in total rapture.

Lord, your divine countenance expresses compassion: through this Lord we can behold that iniquity is completely against you, to the extent that if we encounter with any form of iniquity we shall never behold your countenance. The greater our iniquity is, the greater is our decline from your divine beholding, for as long as the iniquity remains. Our iniquity imparts to us immense grief and anguish, we may even imagine that we are under the threat of expiry, even of hell itself and during this time we cannot behold our rapturous entity that is to come. You have shown, however, Lord that we never expire in your beholding and that you never depart from us. We shall never impart our true honour to you until we find our total rapture in you, genuinely beholding your glorious and divine countenance. This is your ordination for our higher entity imparted through your benevolence.

Lord, the more distinctly that our higher entity beholds your divine countenance, through your devoted benevolence, the more it yearns to behold it completely. Lord, you dwell in us and abide with us, you adopt us and surround us out of compassionate devotion, and shall never depart from us, you are closer to us than anyone can discern, but we never stop lamenting, weeping and yearning till we distinctly discern your gracious divine countenance. In that treasured rapturous beholding no anguish can remain or any bliss depart from us.

Lord, through this you have shown that there is reason for rapture and sorrow; rapture because you Lord our maker are so close to us. You dwell in us and we in you, in total safety through your immense benevolence; and sorrow because our devoted will is short-sighted and we are so burdened with the weight of our temporal entity and the clouding of our iniquity that we cannot distinctly behold your divine countenance. As a consequence of this clouding, we can hardly have faith and accept your immense devotion and our guardianship. That is why we can never stop lamenting and weeping. Our lamenting is not just in our temporal entity but it touches our higher entity. Our higher entity aches with an anguished yearning to behold your gracious blessed countenance, and if it could have everything else but not behold that then it would forever lament and weep. And if, consequently we were in all the anguish that our temporal entity could possibly discern, but at that moment we could behold your glorious divine countenance, then none of the anguish would make us anxious.

Lord, in the moment of that rapturous beholding signifies the expiry of all anguish for the devoted higher entity, and the completion of all bliss and rapture. You showed Lord that you are the one with highest dominion; the one who is immensely humble; you are all entity.

Lord, three forms of discernment are ready for us. The first is discernment of you our Lord God; the second is discernment of our temporal entity, what we are in our lower character and by benevolence; the third is meek discernment of how we have developed in our iniquity and frailty. Amen.

THE SIXTEENTH REVELATION

CHAPTER 73

How there are two types of ailments. One is intolerance or apathy as a consequence of allowing our trials and tribulations bear on us too much, the other is despondency or a distrusting anxiety.

Lord God, Heavenly Father, you have shown there are two types of ailments. One is intolerance or apathy as a consequence of allowing our trials and tribulations bear on us too much, the other is despondency or a distrusting anxiety. Lord, you have shown that these are the two iniquities that weigh on us mostly and agitate us, and you desire those who for devotion of you abhor iniquity and desire to carry out your ordinations, should let them go. In our devout short sight and the apathy of our lower entity we often turn to those iniquities. Lord, it is your ordination that we acknowledge them and turn away from them as we do with other iniquity.

Lord Jesus, to empower us you very tenderly showed your forbearance throughout your grievous Passion. You also showed your bliss and rapture that you took in the Passion because of your devotion. You gave us this as an illustration to follow to empower us to endure our anguish readily and with enlightenment, that imparts immense rapture to you and infinite reward to us. They weigh on us so heavily because of our lack of enlightenment of devotion.

Lord, you have shown that the three entities of the

Trinity (beheld as fortitude, enlightenment and devotion) are all uniform. You however desire our higher entity to have the most enlightenment concerning devotion- all that we behold and all that we have rapture with, you desire us to behold and have rapture in devotion. It is at this point that we have our immense spiritual short sight. We may have faith Lord that you have all dominion and undertake all your ordinations, and that you are all-enlightenment and can undertake all your ordinations; but that you are all-devotion and desire to undertake everything- there we fall down. You have shown Lord that it is this lack of enlightenment that holds back your devoted children.

Lord, when we begin to abhor iniquity and change our undertakings by the laws of Holy Church we behold that we are holding on to a distrusting anxiety that hinders us. This comes to pass when we behold our lower entity and our previous iniquities- or the ones we are caught up in- and we behold that we do not keep our word or keep to the virtue that you imparted to us. We often decline into immense dishonourable and indescribable distress. When we behold this we are so repentant and downcast that we almost do not know where to turn.

Lord, we may describe this anxiety as lowliness, but that is a mistake, and an iniquitous misapprehension. We do not abhor it as the other iniquities because we are unable to acknowledge it since it is imparted directly from the opponent and is against reality.

Lord God, you have shown that of all the characteristics of the divine Trinity, you desire us to follow devotion for our reliance and inspiration: it is devotion that imparts forbearance and enlightenment to us. Lord, in your benevolence you redeem us our iniquity instantly when we atone, so you desire us to redeem our iniquity of unwarranted despondency and mistrusting anxiety. Amen.

THE SIXTEENTH REVELATION

CHAPTER 74

How the apprehension which derives from adoration of our Lord is the only apprehension that imparts rapture to our Lord.

Lord God, Heavenly Father, you have shown that there are four divisions of apprehension. The first, the apprehension of peril overwhelms a man when he is frail. This apprehension imparts benevolence because just like physical ailments or any anguish that is not iniquitous, it empowers to purify him. All anguish of this division empowers a man if it is endured with forbearance.

The second apprehension is apprehension of affliction; through this apprehension a man is shaken and lifted from the clouding of iniquity. The Holy Spirit cannot impart meek fortitude until we have endured this apprehension of affliction, of the expiry of lower entity and of divine opponents. It is this apprehension which leads us to search for the fortitude and forgiveness of you Lord, and consequently this apprehension brings us to you Lord and empowering us to arrive at atonement under the divine intimation of the Holy Spirit.

The third apprehension is distrusting apprehension. This brings us into despondency, Lord it is your desire that we turn it into devotion by giving us discernment of devotion through your benevolence. You desire to turn the hostility of distrust into the affection of essential devotion. Lord, you never have rapture when your children mistrust your benevolence.

The fourth apprehension is that which derives from adoration for you Lord and you have shown this is the only apprehension that imparts rapture to you. It is the most gentle of apprehensions, for the more apprehension that we have; the less we actually endure in the affection of your devotion.

Devotion and apprehension are brothers. Lord our Creator, you have imparted them in us by your benevolence and you shall never withdraw them from us. It is in our essential character to be devoted and by benevolence we are devoted. We have apprehension too in our essential character and by benevolence. Lord, it is essential to your dominion and fatherhood for us to have apprehension, and to your benevolence for us to have devotion. It is essential that we as your attendants and children to have apprehension of you as Lord and Father and to have devotion for you for your benevolence.

Lord, you have shown that though this adoring apprehension and devotion cannot be parted, they are not identical. They are apart in themselves and in their undertakings but you cannot have one without the other. You have shown that the man who in his temporal entity who is devoted also has apprehension, even though he may not be very enlightened of this.

All other apprehensions that come to us- even if it comes under the false appearance of divinity- are not so genuine. This is how we can discern them apart: the apprehension that drives us to turn instantly away from all that is not benevolent, and with all our entity fall against your breast Lord, discerning our frailty and immense yearning, discerning your infinite benevolence and rapturous devotion, looking only for your redemption, holding steadfastly to you- the apprehension that imparts us to undertake all that, comes from your benevolence Lord and is essential, agreeable and genuine. Any apprehension that does not make us do this is either false or defiled.

So this is the answer: to acknowledge both divisions of apprehension and decline the false one.

Lord, you have shown that the apprehension that is imparted to us by the compassionate undertaking of the Holy Spirit is the same whether it is in our temporal entity or before you Lord in your heavenly abode. It is meek, forbearing and totally agreeable. So in our devotion Lord we shall be in your abode and near to you and in our apprehension we shall be meek before you and forbearing- and both are equal. Lord, may we follow you so that we have an adoring apprehension, be devoted to you meekly and have faith in you with all our fortitude, for if we do this our faith is never futile. Lord, the more immense that our faith is, the more we give you rapture and honour. If we lack to impart this adoring apprehension and meek devotion our faith will, while it remains, soon all go amiss. Our Lord of benevolence, may we pray for this offering of adoring apprehension and gentle devotion in our essential character and in our undertaking, for without it Lord no one can give you rapture. Amen.

THE SIXTEENTH REVELATION

CHAPTER 75

How it is God's ordination that in his time we shall discern the purposes for all his undertakings, and we shall behold for infinity why he has allowed all the entity to come to pass.

Lord God, Heavenly Father, you have shown that you can impart all the entity that we desire. Our three requirements are devotion, yearning and compassion. Compassion stems from devotion, guards us in our times of requirement, and yearning which stems from the same devotion, ascends us to our heavenly abode. You crave for humanity to ascend to you, and out of that craving you have ascended your divine ones who now abide in rapture. You are always calling forth, and absorbing, and beckoning your children in their temporal entity.

Lord, you have shown that you have three forms of yearning and they all have one object- and it is the same object for us, by your dominion.

The first is your yearning for us to discern you and to be devoted to you for infinity- and for you to give us discernment in whatever manner is most suitable and rewarding for us. The higher entities that are in your heavenly abode are without anguish and it is your second yearning for us to ascend up into your heavenly abode's bliss and to be like them. On the last day we shall be overflowing from the bliss of your heavenly abode for infinity, this is your third yearning. Our belief has imparted discernment that on that last day all anguish and grief will expire for those who are redeemed. We shall be imparted with the bliss that the higher entities have always obtained in your heavenly abode, and we shall also be imparted with a new bliss that shall stem from you abundantly and shall overflow in us. This has been your benevolent ordination from the beginning of time which are precious and enfolded in you, for all your creatures do not have the fortitude or are devoted enough to be imparted with them until the last day. You have shown that it is your ordination that at that time we shall discern the purposes for all your undertakings and we will behold for infinity why you have allowed all the entity to come to pass. Then our rapture and accomplishment will be so immense and so tall that it will overflow in all your creation with awe and admiration, so that they will have an overflowing feeling of devout awe for you, as never beheld before. It will be so exalted that the very columns of your heavenly abode will quiver and rock! But through this quivering and rocking there will be no anguish at all. Lord, your exalted dominion necessitates that your creatures should behold you in this manner- in immense awe, quivering and rocking in meek rapture as they are amazed at the exaltation of their Lord and Creator and the inconsequence of all your creation. Such a beholding makes your creatures totally meek and mild!

Lord, it is your desire- and is obligatory upon us, both in our essential character and by benevolence- to acknowledge this and discern it for ourselves. We should yearn for such a beholding of you and such an encounter of you to guide us in the right path, guard us in the genuine entity and make us in unison with you. Lord, you are as exalted as you are benevolent; your exaltation necessitates reverence as much as your benevolence must have devotion. Such adoring awe is the affectionate graciousness that is imparted to you in your heavenly abode.

Then you shall be discerned and have sovereign devotion- but you are the same now; then you will be in sovereign awe- and you are no different now. So all your heavenly abode and all your all your earthly creation must quiver and rock when their columns do. Amen.

THE SIXTEENTH REVELATION

CHAPTER 76

How a person in their temporal entity who has beheld the devoted affection of our Lord Jesus abhors iniquity more than hell.

Lord God, Heavenly Father, you have shown that that the higher entities that are in awe of you and that truly acknowledge the discernment of the Holy Spirit abhor the wretchedness and anguish of iniquity more than all the anguish of hell. A person in their temporal entity who has beheld the devoted affection of you Lord Jesus abhors iniquity more than hell. Lord God, you desire us to acknowledge iniquity and pray earnestly, undertake diligently, and look for discernment, so that we do not decline back into iniquity, or if we do go back, are able to depart quickly from it. To turn away from you Lord into iniquity is the most immense anguish anyone can experience in his or her temporal entity.

If we encounter iniquity in another person, we must depart from it as if from the anguish of hell, and we should look to you to empower us against it. Beholding another person's iniquity clouds the eyes of the higher entity. While it remains we cannot behold your grace, unless we behold those iniquities with the sinner's immense remorse, and are overflowing with compassion and to represent him we come to you with a devout yearning. If we do not do this and behold those iniquities we shall be shaken, harmed and held back.

Lord, you have shown that the most enlightened undertaking for a man in his temporal entity is to adhere to your ordinations and teachings Lord Jesus, our highest companion. It is your ordination and you teach us to cling steadfastly to you- at all times, in whatever condition we are in. Whether we are iniquitous or pure, you always behold us as the same in your devotion, whether for benevolence or iniquity, you never desire for us to depart from you. We often decline into iniquity because of our own unfaithfulness and then, in our lack of intellect and spiritual short sight and at the intimation of our opponent, we acquire this distrusting apprehension.

Our opponents magnify this apprehension by emphasising our iniquitous undertaking and reminding us how we promised to try and turn from iniquity. As a consequence we are reluctant to turn to you our affectionate Lord. This is our opponent's undertaking to dispirit us by overflowing us with invalid apprehensions about our baseness and the anguish that he intimidates us with. His desire is to overpower us and grind us down so that we then lose the beholding of the adorable rapturous consideration of you our infinite companion, Lord Jesus. Amen.

THE SIXTEENTH REVELATION

CHAPTER 77

How we should not blame ourselves immensely, or imagine that our tribulations and despair are all our own failing. Our whole temporal entity is an esteemed atonement. Our Lord desires for us to have rapture in the solution that he has imparted to us.

Our benevolent Lord, you have shown the malice of the opponent, that all that is opposed to devotion and repose is akin to the opponent. We often decline into iniquity because of our feeble-mindedness and frailty, but we will always ascend again to more immense bliss, through the compassion and benevolence of the Holy Spirit. It gives our opponent rapture to behold our decline, but this departs by our return to devotion and meekness. This exalted ascension imparts immense misery and anguish that he abounds with continuing jealousy in his abhorrence for us. All the misery that he would impart to us will return to him and you disdain him Lord.

Lord, in our resolution we should be conscious of our weaknesses and cling to you. The more immense that our longing is, the more urgent is our need to stay near to you. We should admit to ourselves that we warrant our anguish. Exalted Lord you may admonish us harshly; you are all enlightenment, and can admonish us with discernment and you are all benevolence and are devoted to us compassionately. We should remain with this perspective. Lord, it is a devoted undertaking of lowliness if we intentionally and readily consent to the tribulation and admonishment that you ordain to impart to us and it is the undertaking of the Holy Spirit's compassion and benevolence in our iniquitous entities. Your admonishment will be meek and light for us to shoulder when we are genuinely content with you Lord

God, Heavenly Father, and with all that you have undertaken.

Lord, you have shown that we should mildly consent and bear the admonishment that you impart to us and concentrate our intellect on your holy Passion. If we undertake this with compassion and devotion, then we endure with you, just as your companions did who beheld it.

Lord, you have shown that we should not blame ourselves immensely, or imagine that our tribulation and despair are all our own failing. You do not desire that we should be excessively downcast and mournful. You have shown that what ever our undertaking is we will encounter some degree of affliction. You desire that we consent to our atonement with enlightenment and to behold that our whole temporal entity is an esteemed atonement.

Lord, our existence in our temporal entity is a confinement and atonement. Lord, you have shown, however, that you desire us to have rapture in the solution that you impart to us- for the solution is that you abide with us, guarding and guiding us into total rapture. It is an overflowing rapture for us to discern that you desire to be our defender in our temporal entity and our genuine bliss when our fundamental entity ascends to your heavenly abode! Our guidance and our heaven stem from genuine devotion and absolute belief. Lord, you have shown this constantly and especially what you have shown of your Passion, where you earnestly desire us to select you as our heaven.

Lord, let us adhere to you and be fortified; adjoin you and be made pure; cleave to you and be impregnable and sheltered from every misfortune.

Our affectionate Lord, you desire us to have the impression that we are as comfortable as our nature can discern or our fundamental entity can yearn for. We should be attentive not to consider this intimate affinity so informally that we do not remember our demeanour. Lord, you are totally affectionate and as gracious as you are affectionate: you are the quintessence of grace. Lord, you desire your devoted children- that will abide with you in your heavenly abode for infinity- to be akin to you in our entire demeanour. Genuine redemption means to be completely akin to you. It is total rapture!

Lord, if we do not have any discernment of how we might undertake this, then we should beseech you and you will impart enlightenment; it is your rapture and gives exaltation to you. We pay homage to you! Amen.

THE SIXTEENTH REVELATION

CHAPTER 78

How God has shown us discernment that though he may exalt us high into reflection through his own unique offering, we must at the same time be conscious of our own iniquity and frailty.

Lord God, heavenly Father, through your benevolence you have shown our iniquity and frailty. As our iniquity is so abominable and abhorrent that out of your immense affection you will only let us behold it by the illumination of your benevolence and forgiveness. In this illumination you have given us enlightenment of four aspects that you desire us to discern. First, you are our foundation from whom we have our complete entity and nature. Second, you guard us mightily and compassionately throughout our iniquity when we are among all our opponents who would crush us: our vulnerability is especially immense because in the short sight of our longing we impart so many openings to our weakness. Third, you give sanctuary to us with the most immense affection and enlighten us when we have strayed from the right path. Fourth, you abide for us, without fluctuating or diversifying, because you desire that we veer again to you, and be in unison with you in devotion, as you are to us.

Lord, if we discern this through your benevolence, we can behold our iniquity assuredly, without being downcast. It is our longing that we should behold it as it genuinely is, though the beholding will empower us to have emotions of shame of our lower entity, and overwhelm us in our arrogance and boldness. We must behold distinctly that in our lower entity we are completely iniquitous and base. From the small portion that you allow us to behold we can speculate how much more our iniquity must be that we do not behold. In your immense compassion you restrict this to what you let us behold- for our iniquity is so impure and abhorrent that we could not truly behold it in its entirety without expiring. But as we meekly come to discern part of our iniquity, we shall have immense remorse, and then Lord in your benevolence you will separate us from all that is not adjoined to you, you will totally restore us and bring us in unison to your entity.

Lord, you have shown that you have ordained this separation and restoration to be for everyone. For the most exalted in his lower entity, the one who is in the most unison with you should behold that he is iniquitous. And the most base in their lower entity can be consoled along with the most exalted because Lord you have brought us in unison in your devotion. Lord, you have shown us discernment that though you may exalt us high into reflection through your own unique offering, yet at the same time we must be conscious of our iniquity and frailty. Otherwise we shall never encounter genuine lowliness, and without that we can never be redeemed.

Lord, you have shown that it is through your devotion, forgiveness and benevolence that you impart this discernment and we are immensely beholden to you. Amen.

THE SIXTEENTH REVELATION

CHAPTER 79

How God has given us discernment that we should focus on our own iniquity, and only behold the iniquity of other people if we can reassure or assist our fellow companions in our Lord Jesus Christ.

Lord God, Heavenly Father, you have shown that all humanity is iniquitous and will remain so to the end of their lower entity. You have given discernment that we should focus on our own iniquity, and only behold the iniquity of other people if we can reassure or assist our fellow- companions in you our Lord Jesus Christ.

Lord, you have shown with immense force and unequivocally, that your devotion is infinite and never fluctuates, and through your immense benevolence and because our fundamental entity is secure in your compassion, our higher entity shall never be separated from your devotion.

Lord, this was meant as an affectionate instruction, an agreeable and merciful communication from you to inspire us. You desire that in the existence of our lower entity we should be in the affable tenderness of your devotion and to discern that all that is in opposition to that both within ourselves and in outside entity, is imparted from our opponent, and not from you Lord God. For instance if we are encouraged to start existing without caution and to pay no attention to the condition of our character because we have encountered your deep devotion Lord, then we should have immense vigilance. If such an encouragement comes, it is not genuine, and we should abhor it, because it is not adjoined to your ordination Lord.

When our short sight or frailty makes us decline into iniquity, then our gracious Lord you direct us, encourage and beseech us. You desire that we behold how base we are and meekly stand up to it. But it is not your desire that we should remain in that condition, overcome with self-blame and floundering in self-commiseration, but you desire us to veer hastily to you. You remain all alone, and remain for us, grievously and overflowing with distress, until we return, and then you hasten to adjoin us back to yourself. For we are your bliss and rapture, and you are our redemption and our entity.

Lord, by showing that you stand alone for us you desire us to discern that this was when you completed your ordination on earth, apart from the divine companions of your heavenly abode. Amen.

THE SIXTEENTH REVELATION

CHAPTER 80

How our Lord has shown that he is the closest and the most accessible, the most exalted and the most inferior; and he will undertake everything. Our Lord Jesus will always bring us out of our affliction, for there cannot be devotion without compassion.

Lord God, Heavenly Father, you have shown that there are three entities that sustain humanity in their temporal entity. With these three, we give you exaltation and you give us assistance, guardianship and redemption.

The first is essential comprehension; the second is day to day discernment of Holy Church; the third is the inner benevolent undertaking of the Holy Spirit. All three come from you Lord: you are the foundation of our essential comprehension; you are the discernment of the Church, you are the Holy Spirit. Each entity is a diverse offering that you desire us to particularly cherish and focus on. Together they are constantly undertaking in us and impart immense entity. You desire us to undertake the first stages in discerning all this in our temporal entity, in a way like beginning to learn to read. This basic understanding, which will end in your heavenly abode, will guide us on our path on earth.

Lord, our belief gives us discernment that you alone- took on our character, also you Lord Jesus- and no one else- undertook all for our redemption. You also undertake everything until the end of time, that is, you reign here with us, have sovereignty and guide us in this temporal entity, and you ascend us up to your heavenly abode. You will carry on this undertaking while any fundamental entity is left on earth who is going to your heavenly abode- even if there were only one fundamental entity left you would remain with him alone till you had ascended him up to your heavenly abode, too.

Lord, you have shown that we should have the belief and the discernment of the council of angels, as the clergy instructs us; but you have also shown that you are the closest and the most accessible, the most exalted and the most inferior; and you undertake everything. You undertake everything that is needed to impart bliss in your heavenly abode, and you undertake everything that is exalted.

Lord, you have shown that you wait for us mournfully and overflowing with distress, you wait for us with genuine emotion that is in our character- the remorse and compassion, distress and heartache that we endure because we are not in unison with you. All three emotions are imparted from you Lord Jesus and are benevolent to us. Lord Jesus, you will always bring us out of our affliction, for there cannot be devotion without compassion.

Lord Jesus, you have shown that whenever we decline into iniquity, and stop contemplating you, and disregard our fundamental entity, then you alone endure all the afflictions, and you stand there downcast and lamenting. It is then up to us, out of immense devotion and from the profoundness of our character, to veer hastily to you Lord Jesus, not to leave you alone.

You reign here on your own with all humanity: you are only here because of us. If we estrange ourselves from you by iniquity, despondency or apathy, then we have undertaken all we can to leave you standing alone. This is how it is with all of us who are iniquitous. But you have shown that however often we undertake this, in your benevolence you never depart from us. You remain with us all the time, and with your most immense affection you absolve us and always screen us from guilt in your beholding. Amen.

THE SIXTEENTH REVELATION

CHAPTER 81

How God beholds us so delicately that he discerns our complete temporal entity as atonement. His devotion makes him yearn for us. All our character yearns for him and this is our perpetual atonement.

Our benevolent Lord, you have shown yourself in different ways both in your heavenly abode and in your temporal entity, but your genuine abode is in man's fundamental entity.

You showed yourself in your temporal entity in the affectionate personification and in your divine Passion here on earth. You have also shown yourself as if you were on a mission- that is, abiding with us, guiding us, and remaining with us, till you have ascended us all to your rapture in your heavenly abode. At different times you have shown your dominion and mostly your dominion is in our fundamental entity. You have created this entity as your abiding place and your sovereign city and you have ordained that you shall never depart that exalted throne.

Your dwelling abode is awesome and noble, and you desire us to acknowledge hastily to your direction of benevolence, having exultation in your unimpaired devotion instead of having distress over our habitual decline into iniquity.

Out of all the undertakings that we can impart to show our distress for our iniquity, we give you the most immense exaltation by living happily and joyfully because of your devotion. For you behold us so delicately that you discern our complete temporal entity as atonement. All our character yearns for you and this is our perpetual atonement: it is an atonement that you have created in us, and in your benevolence you assist us to shoulder it. Your devotion makes you yearn for us; your enlightenment, validity and virtue make you remain for us while we are in our temporal entity; and you desire to behold this yearning and waiting in us. Lord, you have ordained that this is our essential atonement- and our most immense atonement, too. And you have ordained that this atonement shall never depart from us until we are totally pure and have you for our honour. Therefore Lord, you have shown that you desire us to direct our inclination on our transient journey from the anguish we experience over into the rapture that we believe in. Amen.

THE SIXTEENTH REVELATION

CHAPTER 82

How God has shown that when we decline and ascend again we are immensely cherished by him and guarded by the same devotion.

Lord God, Heavenly Father, you have shown all the lamenting and sorrow that is in our fundamental entity. You have clarified that you are immensely conscious that we desire to exist for your devotion, and that for this we blissfully and cheerfully bear all the atonement that may be imparted to us. As we cannot exist without iniquity, for consideration of your devotion we are prepared to endure all the sorrow, agitation and anguish that may be imparted to us. And this is genuine. But you desire that we should not be too agitated by the iniquity that we undertake without real intention.

Lord, you have shown that you behold your children with compassion instead of condemnation. In our transient entity on earth you discern that we will not exist completely without condemnation and iniquity. You are devoted to us infinitely though we continually are iniquitous and very tenderly you show yourself to us. It is then that we softly lament and have sorrow, turning to behold your compassion, adhering to your devotion and benevolence, discerning that you are our cure, acknowledging that we undertake nothing but iniquity. Then in the humbleness that comes in beholding our iniquity we believe you and encounter your infinite devotion, giving you gratitude and exaltation- and so we impart rapture to you. Lord, you have shown that you are devoted to us and we are devoted to you, and our devotion will not be separated into two. You permit all this to assist us.

Lord, you have ordained that you will keep us protected and unimpaired.

Our holy Lord, you yearn for us to exist in longing and bliss- and all that is not adjoined to you is imparted from the opponent. You desire that we should acknowledge this in the affectionate benevolent enlightenment of your fundamental devotion. You have shown that when we decline and ascend again we are immensely cherished by you and are guarded by the same devotion. Lord, in your beholding we do not decline, and in our own beholding we do not prevail. Both of these beholding are genuine, but your beholding is the exalted reality. We are immensely grateful to you because you want us to discern this exalted reality while we are still in our lower entity. You have shown that while we are in our lower entity it assists us to behold both of these realities together. This exalted reality consoles our fundamental entity and keeps us having bliss in you Lord, while the inferior beholding keeps us apprehensive and makes us humiliated of our lower entity.

Our benevolent Lord, you have shown that it is your desire that we give much greater consideration to the exalted reality, while not departing from the inferior, until the moment when we are ascended to your heavenly abode. Lord Jesus, there you will be our honour and we shall be overflowing with exaltation and rapture for infinity. Amen.

THE SIXTEENTH REVELATION

CHAPTER 83

How the attributes of God are entity, devotion and enlightenment.

Lord God, Heavenly Father, you have shown three of your attributes- and on these rely the dominion and validity of all that you have shown. They are present in all that you have shown, but principally in the Twelfth showing, where you often showed that you are the one.

These attributes are entity, devotion and enlightenment.

In our entity there is a miraculous affability; in devotion, an affectionate benevolence; and in enlightenment genuine character is beheld for infinity. These attributes abide as benevolence: and our intellect desires to be affiliated to this benevolence, and to adhere to it with all its fortitude.

Lord, we should behold this in devout awe and be overflowing with admiration at what you have ordained to show us and at the discernment of affectionate accord that is imparted to us when our discernment is in you. We should discern that this is the most exalted offering that we can gain, and its foundation is in essential character.

Our belief is an enlightenment, which passes simply from out of our infinite day- that, is from you our Father, Lord God. By this enlightenment our Mother, you our Lord Jesus Christ, and our benevolent Lord, the Holy Spirit, guide us through this transitory lower entity. You give a portion of this enlightenment to each of us, and this is ready to satisfy our yearnings in the night. From your enlightenment you impart our entity; from the night all our anguish and sorrow- but it is as a result of this anguish and sorrow that we attain the honour and gratitude of you Lord God. Through your forgiveness and benevolence we resolutely discern and believe our enlightenment, following it perceptively with all our fortitude.

Lord, when our sorrow ceases, at once our eyes in the illuminated daylight shall behold with complete clarity- and this enlightenment is you, our Lord God, our Creator, and the Holy Spirit, in you, Lord Jesus Christ our redeemer.

Lord God, you desire us to behold and discern that our belief is our illumination in the dark night, and this illumination is in you our God, our infinite day. Amen.

THE SIXTEENTH REVELATION

CHAPTER 84

How the enlightenment of God is devotion.

Lord God, Heavenly Father, the enlightenment is devotion, which in your discernment you give us a portion, which is most beneficial to us.

The enlightenment does not impart sufficient illumination to empower us to behold our most blissful day, but neither is that day completely concealed. We have enough enlightenment to live a fruitful entity of arduous undertaking that attains the infinite exaltation of you Lord. This was beheld in the sixth showing, where you declared that you impart gratitude for all our assistance and arduous undertaking. So devotion keeps us in our belief and anticipation, and the anticipation guides us in devotion. And finally all will be devotion.

Lord, you desire us to discern this devotion in three ways. First uncreated devotion; second, created devotion; third imparted devotion. *Uncreated devotion* is you Lord; *created devotion*; is our fundamental entity in you Lord; *imparted devotion*; is righteousness. Imparted devotion is a cherished offering, which you undertake in us Lord. Through this we are devoted to you Lord for yourself, we are devoted to ourselves in you Lord; and we are devoted to all the entity that you are devoted to, on your behalf. Amen.

THE SIXTEENTH REVELATION

CHAPTER 85

How God's children in unison give him exaltation. Because it is like this: all is agreeable.

Lord God, Heavenly Father, you have shown that irrespective of our foolishness and short sight here in our temporal entity, in your affection you are constantly beholding us, and having rapture in your undertaking. Out of all that we can undertake, we can impart the most immense rapture by perceptively and genuinely trusting this and by having bliss being in unison with you and in you.

Lord, you have ordained that assuredly we shall one day discover ourselves in the infinite rapture of you, giving you exaltation and giving our gratitude. So it is assured that before all entity you beheld us, were devoted to us and discerned us, and we were a portion of your infinite ordination. In your ageless devotion you created our entity, and in that same devotion you guard us and you will never permit us to be impaired in any manner that will imperil our infinite rapture.

Lord, when your determination is proclaimed and we are all ascended to your heavenly abode, we shall distinctly behold in you the enigmas that are now concealed from us. Then none of your children will have any inclination to declare that if things had been different, then it would have been superior. Rather all your children shall declare in unison; we give you exaltation, Lord, because it is like this: all is agreeable. We can now genuinely behold that all has been undertaken just as you ordained it before any entity was created Lord. Amen.

THE SIXTEENTH REVELATION

CHAPTER 86

How God has given us enlightenment that all his declaration to us was his devotion to us.

Lord God, Heavenly Father, let us all pray for devotion. Lord, with you undertaking in us, let us give you exaltation, believe and have rapture in you. Our benevolent Lord, you have shown that it is your desire that we discern that this is how we should pray to you- you have declared that you are the foundation of our supplication.

Lord, you genuinely desire us to behold and discern that you have shown us all this because you desire for it to be more understood than it is. And as we come to discern it you will impart benevolence to be devoted to you and to adhere to you. You behold your heavenly prize on earth with immense devotion that you desire to bring our essential character to you, departing from the grief and despondency we abide in, and impart to us greater enlightenment and consolation in the rapture of your heavenly abode.

Lord, you desire us to discern through all you have shown that your devotion was your declaration to us. It was devotion that showed it to us. It was devotion that we were shown. Devotion was the reason that you showed it. You have ordained that if we remain with this devotion we shall discern more about devotion, but we shall never ever discern anything else from it.

Lord, you have given us enlightenment that all your declaration to us was your devotion to us.

Lord, you have shown with total assurance that before you created us you were devoted to us, and your devotion has never diminished, and never will. In your devotion you have imparted all your undertakings for our blessing, and in this devotion we shall have our entity for infinity. Through your making of us we had an inception, but the devotion with which you created us never had an inception: it was in this devotion that we had our inception.

All this we shall behold in you our Lord God, for infinity. Amen.

Postscript

By the scribe who probably wrote this book out for Julian.

Lord Jesus accede us this. Amen.

So concludes the declarations of devotion of the divine Trinity shown by our Saviour Christ Jesus for our infinite consolation and restoration and so that we may have bliss in him in this transient temporal pilgrimage. Amen, Jesus, Amen.

Lord God, Heavenly Father, I pray that this book may only be imparted to those who will be your devoted believers, who will acknowledge the belief of Holy Church and abide by the righteous creed and discernment of men who are benevolent, prepared and of orthodox education. For this declaration is comprised of such intense doctrine and enlightenment that it can have nothing to declare to anyone in their temporal entity who is in bondage to iniquity and the opponent.

Lord, we should guard against selecting and preferring one thing that attracts us and departing from another- for that is what a dissenter does. But we should accede to every portion and genuinely discern that it concurs with your divine word Lord, and has its foundation in it. And Lord Jesus our devotion, enlightenment and validity you will impart this to all innocent fundamental entities whom meekly and devoutly beseech you for discernment.

And those who have gained this book give genuine gratitude to our Lord Jesus Christ, with all your emotion, for imparting all those declarations and showings. In his infinite devotion, forgiveness and benevolence he imparted them to you and for you, to be a faithful direction for all of us in our lower entity, to guide us to infinite rapture. I pray that Jesus may accede us this. Amen.

EXPLANATION OF THE SIXTEEN VISIONS GIVEN TO JULIAN OF NORWICH.

How did these visions come about? While Julian was still living at home she had desired three gifts of God. The first was understanding of Christ's Passion, the second was bodily sickness; the third was to have of God's gift three wounds. The wound of contrition, the wound of kind compassion, and the wound of wilful longing towards God.

When she became so ill that her curate was sent for, he set before her a cross. As she gazed upon the cross all the pain was taken from her body.

As she continued to set her eyes upon the cross our Lord showed his first vision. It was as though she was seeing the cross as it was at the time of our Lord's Passion. Blood flowed down from under his crown of thorns. She saw he who was God made man suffered in this way for her.

Then suddenly the Trinity swelled her heart with unfathomable devotion. She saw that in the presence of our Lord Jesus there is always the presence of God, our creator and guardian. The Trinity is our infinite devotion, rapture and blessedness. She was engulfed with amazement that our Lord Jesus, so divine and wondrous would come into the unrighteous presence of her shameful temporal entity and be so warm and friendly to her.

Then our Lord desired for her to behold Mary as she was in her human body, a pure meek virgin, hardly more than a child was. He desired for her to discern of her insight and devotions, her absolute fascination that the creator should be born from her, someone so humble, whom God had made. Our Lord showed that assuredly in benevolence and righteousness she is greater to the entirety of God's creation, save his greater benevolence, our blessed Saviour and companion.

From this vision of the Trinity it gave Julian comprehension of the Incarnation, and the union between God and man's soul. All the wonderful revelations about eternal wisdom and love, which followed this, were based on this and held together in this.

Then our Lord showed her what looked like a fragile hazelnut in the palm of her hand, and it was as small as a ball. He showed her that this is all creation that he possesses in his mercy. He showed how small creation is compared to God who is uncreated. As we are an element of his divine creation we can only find pure repose in him who is the creator, guardian and beloved. Our Lord showed Julian that all the revelations were for all her fellow companions in him.

In the Second Revelation he showed the blemishing of his face on the cross which was made for our atonement. He showed that through his Holy Passion he takes away the disgrace of our degrading acts. God out of his benevolent mercy created man, by that same devotion he desired to return him to that condition of blessedness and bestow on him even greater ecstasy. He made us like the Trinity at our first creation but desired for us to be like our beloved Saviour Lord Jesus and abide forever in heaven, by the capability of our re-creation. Our Lord Jesus through these two creations pronounced to come into this temporal life of death, with all its deplorable defilement. He did this through his tender and merciful devotion for his creation. He showed that he has great rapture when we forever look for him.

In the Third Revelation he showed Julian that he is in the centre of all living things and through him he does all things that is righteous except sin.

In the Fourth Revelation our Lord showed that we have an immense reserve of water to make us contented in our temporal life. But that it is in his plentiful, precious, beloved blood that he wishes to cleanse us from our iniquities, so that the blood becomes an element of us. Just as it can cleanse all in the world that desire to be cleansed from iniquity, so it also streams for infinity through the heavens.

In the Fifth Revelation our Lord showed that his Holy Passion has conquered the enemy. The enemy still strives to be as vengeful as he was before the Personification of our Lord Jesus. The enemy has to observe with anguish, humility and abhorrence the redeemed souls flee from him to our Lord God. Our Lord desires for us to follow his example and spurn the enemy's evil intent.

In the Sixth Revelation our Lord Jesus showed how our Lord God Heavenly Father imparts his three offerings of gratitude to his adored companions in his heavenly abode, and every man will be rewarded for his willing service and the length of his service. Our divisions of rapture in his heavenly abode will be firstly the redeemed soul whose tribulation is ended. The second division of rapture is that he will impart to the company of heaven the work that each soul has done for him. The third division of rapture is that the original natural delight with which it is first imparted will never languish.

In the Seventh Revelation our Lord showed that we are imparted with encouragement through our times of well being and depression. He keeps our soul protected in pleasant and distressing times alike and his blessedness will last forever for those who are going to be redeemed.

In the Eighth Revelation our Lord revealed his last pains in the expiring of his Passion. His face was transformed through his slow agonizing death. The fluids in his body withered so much that it appeared that he had been dead for seven nights.

In the Ninth Revelation our Lord revealed the abiding benevolence for mankind that brought him to his Passion and how this spread throughout the heavens. He revealed that if he could have suffered more he would have done so. As we are Jesus' eternal crowns it gives him infinite rapture, and so he disregards all his torment and grievous anguish, his excruciating and humiliating death. He also revealed that it is his will that we share immense bliss with him in our atonement and that we seek blessing of him that we may do so. He desires no other reward.

In the Tenth Revelation our Lord revealed that his heart was sundered in two for the benevolence of mankind. He showed his wounded side with bliss. He wants us to know that in his side there is an adorable heavenly abode, vast enough for every person who is going to be redeemed to have tranquility in serenity and benevolence.

In the Eleventh Revelation our Lord revealed a beholding of Mary his sanctified Mother. He revealed her at the time of his Passion. He showed himself looking down from his cross and her standing there. He showed that she is his inestimable pleasure and exaltation. For our devotion for us he elevated her and enabled her to be so eminent.

In the Twelfth Revelation our Lord taught that he is the one, that until we abide with him we will never find true repose. He is the one we yearn for. He is the one of all bliss, affability, kindness, unsurpassed happiness and existence itself.

In the Thirteenth Revelation Julian wondered why in God's knowledge his discernment allowed the origin of iniquity to exist. Our Lord answered to Julian that iniquity is inescapable, but that all will be agreeable and every aspect will be agreeable. He wanted us to discern that we cannot see iniquity itself. It has no entity or materiality in us and can only be discerned through the anguish it creates. Iniquity is the creator of all anguish. He also taught that in God there is an incomprehensible enigma concerning the origin of iniquity. When we are enfolded with God in heaven, we shall truly discern why he permitted iniquity to occur. He revealed that our suffering in sin would be converted in heaven into something exalted, into eternal blessing and infinite bliss. He depleted himself in his Holy Passion to not only bring us into exaltation but that we are to have solace in our anguish. As his blessed children he desires us to restrain from grieving and being broken hearted about our own anguishes through his absolving, consideration and compassion.

He revealed that the gravest iniquity that has ever been committed or ever will be committed was Adam's iniquity. He desires us to behold the exalted recompense he has achieved for iniquity. This has brought God greater bliss than Adam's iniquity has brought him.

He desires for us not to dwell on iniquity but to discern that through the Holy Trinity all will be agreeable. All living souls on earth cannot know how and when the last act of the divine Trinity will take place, it is cherished and concealed within the divine domain of God.

He revealed that the entity that is iniquitous he tolerates. He bestows compassion and benevolence through the lowliness of his undertaking, by which we can discern his righteousness. This compassion will endure as long as iniquity is tolerated tormenting souls. The entity will be brought into righteousness for eternity. Our Lord Jesus tolerates us descending into iniquity but our higher entity is kept secure in his forgiveness and benevolence. It will be the most immense delight to behold the act that our Lord God will accomplish.

When we veer to what is denounced we should discern that we should veer back to our Lord Jesus beseeching him for forgiveness and benevolence. Through our affliction, distress and immense torment we discern our own fragility and the suffering our iniquity creates for us.

He revealed that there is a debased side to our character that cannot desire what is benevolent. But there is also a divine desire, which is our elevated character, which has never given consent to iniquity, or will ever do so for infinity.

He revealed, however, that although iniquity is forgiven it is the harshest scourge with which his elected living souls can be chastised. The Holy Spirit guides us to sincerely acknowledge our iniquities. Then we are ransomed from iniquity and anguish.

He revealed that there are three phases that a soul can enter his heavenly domain. By remorse we are made pure; by tenderness we are made ready; by devoted yearning we are made deserving of him. He revealed through his compassion that he desires that the devoted souls should not be despondent because they so frequently and harshly descend into iniquity. Our descending into iniquity does not impede his devotion for us. He enfolds us from our foes that assail us so ruthlessly and maliciously.

Our Lord revealed that true love alone should make us abhor iniquity; there is no more immense hell than iniquity for the devoted soul. As he never parts from us in our iniquity because of his devotion, so he desires us not to part our devotion from our fellow companions in their iniquity.

In the Fourteenth Revelation our Lord revealed how our Lord God is the domain of our prayer: he entreats us to pray and imparts all that is essential. Our Lord requires and desires our prayers even when we have no inclination. For even in our arid, barren, feeble and low times our prayer is immensely agreeable to him.

He also revealed that appreciation is essential to prayer. He guides us to veer with all our fortitude to the undertaking he is entreating us to accomplish. Through his dominion his word is imparted to the soul. He beholds that the most blissful appreciation we can impart to him is to delight in him.

It is his desire that our prayers and faith are immense. We can be sure that if we pray to our Lord with conviction for pardon and benevolence, he shall firstly give his compassion and benevolence to us. Through prayer our Lord may command and direct us in our temporal life. We should not become dispirited or uncertain if we do not discern that God is accomplishing things, equally we should pray when we do discern God's accomplishments.

He also revealed that prayer unites the soul to him. Through prayer our soul aspires to the Lord's aspirations. We should have total faith that he shall bestow our earthly longings. He desires that we be joined in his devoted acts. Nothing gives him greater rapture than for us to implore him to ordain his will. This develops our soul in conformity with God. He shows himself to our souls. For a time we will be able to pray for nothing but what he inspires us to pray for. The more our souls discern him, the more it longs for him. He revealed that he will always be perceptive to our souls when we feel stricken, reviled, and feel abandoned in wretchedness.

He is our guide in our longing to pray, encouraging us in

our aspirations. He constantly imparts his acts in many spheres. We should earnestly aspire to be totally in unison with him. Through the Holy Spirit he will impart affectionate spiritual enlightenment and perception. He can intensify his creation above its capacity; to be imparted a higher beholding of him, as Julian experienced. This is in accordance with what our natural character can behold.

Our Lord revealed that although we are iniquitous there is no wrath in God. He is only benevolence, devotion and tranquility. His virtue and righteousness do not permit him to be wrathful. He showed that as our soul is so absolutely affiliated to him in his benevolence, that nothing could separate us.

He revealed that the only wrath and lack of benevolence is in us and he has absolved us of that, through his mercy and compassion. The foundation of forgiveness in us is devotion. His affectionate contemplation and devotion never moves apart from us despite our iniquity.

His forgiveness is understanding- it is shown in the delicate devotion of a mother. His forgiveness gives sanctuary; it adopts us, renews us, and cures us. He converts our appalling shortcoming into abundant and continuous solace; our base decline into exalted recovery and our piteous expiring into righteous sacred entity. Our wrath is hushed and banished by his compassion and forgiveness.

In our Lord's beholding the soul, which is going to be redeemed, has never expired and never will expire. He showed that he associates no greater condemnation to us than to the virtuous and righteous angels in his heavenly abode.

Our Lord then revealed the parable of a master with an attendant. The attendant goes to complete his master's wishes. He falls into a deep pit and is grievously harmed. He makes the mistake of lamenting on his emotions and so he has anguish. The master beholds the attendant with tenderness, lowliness, immense mercy and understanding. His master discerns that he should compensate him for his suffering and add a more immense reward than he has ever had.

This revelation of the master was the Lord God and the attendant was Adam. Our Lord discerns all humanity as one and their decline as one. He has mercy and understanding for the decline of his divine creation; Adam; the bliss and rapture are for his divine Son who is identical to him.

Man's soul is the Lord's own city and abode. His divine Son has restored the city to a place of immense blessing again. When Adam declined (which is all humanity), our Lord Jesus fell into the Virgin's womb to relinquish Adam from all condemnation in his heavenly abode and on earth. Our righteousness and benevolence are imparted from our Lord Jesus, our shortcomings and lack of vision from Adam.

Our heavenly Father revealed that he does not resolve to condemn mankind anymore than he would condemn his beloved Son. For all those souls that are going to be redeemed through Jesus' divine manifestation and Passion is enfolded in Christ's humanity; he is the head and we are the elements of his body.

After our Lord Jesus had fallen into the Virgin's womb he could never ascend once more in all his domain until his humanity had been destroyed, had expired, and had submitted his soul into the dominion of God, alongside with all humanity to whom he had been sent.

Our ascended Lord Jesus abides in us, alongside the baseness and injury as a result of Adam's decline and expiring. Through all our trials and tribulations he is always beside us, guiding us.

Of mankind our Lord revealed that dwelling in every soul that is going to be redeemed there is a godly desire that has never succumbed to iniquity, or ever will. This will is securely enfolded in or Lord Jesus Christ. Mankind's devoted character will eventually furnish his heavenly abode. This devoted character is formed from the Holy Spirit, created by God and enfolded by him, in unison with his character.

He revealed that our faith is a righteousness that is imparted from our inborn fundamental entity into our carnal character through the Holy Spirit. It is a belief that our Lord abides in us and we in him. Through this righteousness our Lord imparts immense acts in us through the dominion of the Holy Spirit.

Our Lord Jesus is our redeemer, we are enfolded in him and always shall be, and so he is our Mother to our fundamental entity, in which we have our foundation. He also became our Mother to our temporal character that he took out of his forgiveness. Our Lord Jesus reciprocates benevolence for iniquity, and so is our genuine Mother, we have all our entity from him, the foundation and beginning of all Motherhood. He is our genuine Mother in benevolence because he took our lower character.

Our Lord enfolds us in devotion and the labour pains he endured were the most excruciating anguishes and the cruelest birth pains imaginable, until the lower entity that he taken on had expired. This was our spiritual birth, our re-creation, out of devotion for our higher character.

With regard to our spiritual birth, he takes care of us with supreme gentleness as he beholds our soul as so valuable. He desires us to turn to him as a small child would turn to its mother for comfort, whenever it needed it.

It is in our fundamental character to abhor iniquity. If we live in unison with our fundamental character and benevolence, we should genuinely behold that iniquity is far worse and gives greater anguish than hell itself, for iniquity is utterly against our gracious fundamental character. We cannot ascend above the condition of a child, until our Lord Jesus, our devoted Mother, ascends us up into our Father's rapture.

In the Fifteenth Revelation our Lord revealed that on the point of expiry of our lower entity through death our redeemed higher entity ascends as a glorious creature, a small child, in all perfection and purer than a lily, that floats up to the heavenly abode. He showed that the expiry of the temporal entity and the decomposition of the body represent the immense iniquity of our temporal existence, and the small child represents the total innocence of our higher entity. This is his gracious, tender, affectionate promise of total release.

Our honour for him should be a devout esteemed awe in unison with graciousness, which is imparted when we behold him as supremely exalted and ourselves as supremely minute. He desires that we be in no awe of any entity but him.

He revealed he has the prominent position in the middle of our higher entity, where he has tranquility and repose and that he will never depart his city. Our higher entity cannot find repose in anything but him.

We may have an arduous passing, we may have affliction;

and we may have trials, but we shall not be conquered in our temporal entity. We should be resolute and fearless, through the agreeable and disagreeable periods of our temporal entity.

He does not impart a greater benevolence that ascends more than faith, and there is no guidance in anything that is beneath it. We should always remain in our faith and cleave to it.

We should let go of any distrusting anxiety over our iniquity and not lament over our past iniquities. Otherwise we are holding on to what hinders us. This in turn becomes an iniquity that we do not recognize, of unwanted despondency. This is imparted directly from the opponent and is against reality. The reality is that in his benevolence our Lord redeems us our iniquity instantly when we atone. The only apprehension we should have is that which derives from adoration of him. In our apprehension we should be meek and forbearing, coupled with devotion. If we do this faith is never futile.

He desires that we should not blame ourselves immensely, or imagine that our tribulation or despair is our own failing. We are to behold that our whole temporal entity is an esteemed atonement. He desires us to adhere to him and be fortified. If we adjoin him we will be made pure. If we cleave to him we will be made impregnable and sheltered from every misfortune. This is genuine redemption.

Although he may exalt us high into reflection through his own unique offering, we must at the same time be conscious of our iniquity and fragility. He gave discernment that we should only behold the iniquity of other people if we can reassure or assist our fellow companions in him. He will always bring us out of affliction because he beholds his children with compassion and pity.

Our Lord's three attributes are entity, devotion and enlightenment. Our faith is an enlightenment, which simply passes out of him, our infinite day. Our Lord Jesus and the Holy Spirit guide us through this transitory lower entity. This enlightenment is devotion. We are given enough enlightenment to live a fruitful entity of arduous undertaking that gives his infinite exaltation. For this he imparts his gratitude.

His children are in unison with him, giving him exaltation. In his heavenly abode we shall behold the enigmas that are now concealed from us. When we behold these in him we will not consider if things could have been different or superior. Rather we shall declare in unison, all is agreeable.

Our Lord finally revealed that all that had been shown was because he desired for it all to be understood more than it was. He desires us to discern that all he showed in his declaration was for his love to us. It was love that showed it to us. It was love that we were shown. Love was the reason that he showed it. He showed with total assurance that before he created us he was devoted to us, and his devotion has never diminished, and never will. She categorically states in chapter sixty-eight that our Lord Jesus said to Julian that it was not through raving that she saw the visions but through him.

Julian is considered to have been a mystic. Mysticism is defined as an experience of a reality beyond normal human understanding or experience. The use of prayer and contemplation is an attempt to achieve direct intuitive experience of the divine. Mystics are conscious of the Lord's spiritual presence in their higher entity. They behold, encounter, and observe our Lord in his undertakings and particularly in the higher entity. They gain a perfect assurance after a period of validation. They find themselves at once discerning as the new mind dictates, beholding and undertaking according to his will. They have compassion of infinite benevolence, without returning to their former nature. They discern God in his benevolence, high and mighty, but also wishing to draw them to himself through his friendly, kind, devoted, affectionate Motherly benevolence. They become as a trusting child, it is in this trust, no matter what befalls them, that our Lord imparts discernment of the divine, an intensified awareness of truth.

In the Second Revelation chapter ten Julian wrote that our Lord Jesus showed that all might seek this union with him. He beseeches his companions to search for him with a devout aspiration, so that we may behold him with utmost bliss. He desires that we behold him with eyes of devotion, even if we may only have a small personal manifestation of him. It gives our Lord great rapture when we forever look for him, agonize and believe in him. This is the action of the Holy Spirit on our inborn desire in our soul. He revealed that through this temporal striving, searching is as good as beholding. May we fulfil his desire to go on looking until we behold him, when he shows himself through his benevolence?

It is only our iniquity that prevents his divine beholding. He still dwells in us and abides with us, but we will never stop lamenting and yearning till our higher entity discerns his gracious divine enlightenment. This, however, is not the beatific vision; we will not behold that until our lower entity has expired.

Julian's book, "Revelations of Divine Love" is as relevant in our turbulent times as it was in her day. We may question if God is all benevolent, all devotion, why is the world in the state that it is in. But despite the iniquity, suffering and evil in the world God has accomplished the victory of Christ over Satan, iniquity and death. He worked his will through Christ who was God made man; he now works through man in his undertakings of benevolence in the power of the Holy Spirit. He has revealed that all will be agreeable, and all manner of things will be agreeable. He shall perform one last immense undertaking that will remain an enigma until it is undertaken. This undertaking will transform all that is not well now, that is contrary to his will. Her revelations reveal that iniquity does not have to be the final stage of our life. We can veer from iniquity and use our gifts in our Lord's service. We can have complete faith in God with his peace and assurance.

Lightning Source UK Ltd.
Milton Keynes UK
16 June 2010

155628UK00001B/8/P